ELIZABETH: A BABY BLESSING

AMISH SECRET BABY

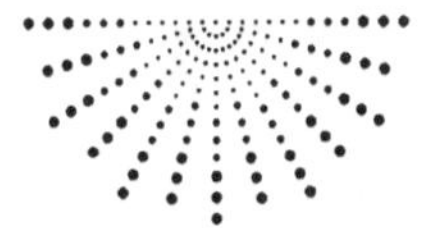

SARAH MILLER

One thing my readers have been asking for is a mini-series of interlinked books. I went back through all my memories and came up with the idea of these three stories all linked with a secret baby.

What could be better as the summer sets in than to sit and read about the amazing Amish and a wonderful baby miracle?

Enjoy these books,

Sarah

For occasional FREE books and to hear about my latest releases join my newsletter here

CHAPTER ONE

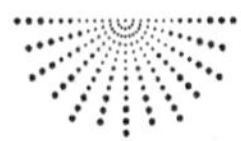

FAITH'S CREEK, PENNSYLVANIA.

"Come on, Leah, you're missing out on the singing," Miriam called from the barn door.

Leah wiped her eyes on her sleeve, glancing at Sarah Beiler, the Bishop's *fraa*.

Sarah smiled at her and patted her arm. "It's all right, go on, but if you want to talk about this some more, my door's always open. Don't forget that," she said.

Feeling a touch of relief, Leah nodded. "Thank you, Sarah – for everything," she said.

"Oh, hurry, Leah, you're missing it all," Miriam called out to her again.

Leah turned and hurried back across the farmyard, hoping her friend would not notice her tear-stained face. "I'm here, don't worry," she said.

Miriam's eyes narrowed and she tilted her head.

Evidently, her attempts at disguising her grief were to no avail.

Catching her by the arm, Miriam pulled her to one side. "Are you all right? You've been crying," she said.

Leah swallowed hard, fighting back her emotions, which were ready to overwhelm her again. She had opened her heart to Sarah Beiler and told her secrets she had never thought she would reveal to another soul. But she was not ready to tell them to Miriam, or to anyone else, and she shook her head, blushing, as Miriam repeated her words.

"I'm all right," Leah said, though it was clear she was not.

"No, you're not, you're really not. Come on now, I know you don't always tell me everything, but I'll listen, I might not be as old as you, but we've been friends long enough to trust one another, haven't we?" she said.

Leah gave a weak smile. Miriam was sixteen, yet to set off on her rumspringa – though desperate to do so. Leah was twenty, but she, Miriam, and Alma had long been friends, as close as sisters, and had shared much together. Now Leah brushed a tear from her eyes and sighed, wishing she could avoid the subject of the secret she had just shared with Sarah Beiler.

"It's just... something that happened on my rumspringa," she said.

Miriam gave her a knowing look. "Oh, I see. What happens on the rumspringa stays on the rumspringa. That sort of thing, is it? Well, I'm sorry I've not experienced it yet. I'm obviously too immature to help someone in need," she said.

Leah shook her head. "It's not that, Miriam, it's just... well, all this stuff with Alma and the *boppli*," she said. A sense of guilt welled up inside of her at how she had behaved in the previous weeks since Alma's return from Philadelphia.

"You behaved pretty badly, but she's forgiven you, hasn't she? Don't hold onto guilt, isn't that what Bishop Beiler says?" Miriam replied.

Leah nodded, thankful for her friend. "It's not about guilt, it's just... oh... I know how Alma feels, that's all. But I don't want to talk about it anymore," she said, pulling away from Miriam, who looked at her in confusion.

"You know how she feels? About looking after another woman's *boppli*?" she asked, her eyes widening in surprise.

Leah nodded.

"But how? What are you hiding, Leah?" Miriam asked, but at that moment, they were interrupted by a voice to their side.

It was Jonathan Kemp, a young man from Faith's Creek, the son of one of the farming families. He was a handsome boy, with brown hair and deep blue eyes, tall and well-built, and who now smiled at them both as Leah blushed.

"Am I interrupting you?" he asked.

Leah shook her head. "Not at all," she said, thankful that he had done just that.

"Oh, good, it's just... well, the dessert is nearly all gone, and you'll miss out on it if you don't come now. Shall I get you some, Miriam?" he asked.

Miriam smiled. "Oh, you don't have to do that," she said, but Jonathan insisted on escorting her back inside the barn, where the festivities continued.

Jonathan had always had a soft spot for Miriam, and at eighteen he would be the perfect match for her. He would often appear unexpectedly, offering to escort her here or there, delighting in bringing her presents or small tokens of his affection. It was sweet, and Leah now took her chance to escape from Miriam's further questioning, slipping away before Miriam could stop her.

"I'll see you later," she called out.

"Oh, but, Leah... wait," Miriam replied, but Leah was gone.

She had no desire to return to the festivities – she would not be missed – so she made her way along the lane from the farm, pausing by a gate that looked out over the corn-fields toward the horizon. The evening was drawing in, the sun setting large and red over the mountains beyond. Leah sighed, glad to have unburdened herself of her secret to Sarah Beiler, knowing it would go no further than that. It felt as if a weight had been lifted off her shoulders, not all of it, but some at least. She put her hands together and began to pray – she had often found herself praying in the weeks gone by – asking *Gott* to guide her in what was to come.

"I need a sign, I need to know what to do," she whispered, feeling the burden of her troubles, and wishing that like Miriam, they only extended as far as dessert...

"THERE'S so many to choose from. I think I'll have a slice of shoofly pie, it's my favorite," Miriam said, glancing distractedly back at the barn door.

She had wanted to discover more about what was troubling Leah, being confused to find her so upset. It frustrated her to always be treated as the younger one, assumed by Leah and Alma to know nothing of the world around her. But Miriam knew more than either of her friends realized, and she could tell something was troubling Leah and her worries troubled her deeply.

"Do you want cream with that?" Jonathan asked.

Brought back to the present, Miriam nodded. "Oh, just a little, please," she said, as he smiled at her. "I should probably go and find Leah..." she said.

Jonathan looked disappointed.

Miriam knew he had a soft spot for her, and she liked him, too, though perhaps not as much as he liked her. He was sweet and always kind. She felt guilty for wanting to slip away, but she was concerned for Leah and anxious to discover more about what was troubling her.

"Don't you want to be here? Alma's your best friend, isn't she?" Jonathan said.

"That's right, but she doesn't need me here now. Besides, they'll be finishing up soon," she said, glancing across the barn to where Alma and Sawyer were singing.

Miriam was pleased for her friend. She liked Sawyer, and it was clear that he and Alma were in love. She took the dish of dessert that Jonathan offered her, and the two of them sat at the side of the barn, watching as the singing continued.

"Was Leah all right?" Jonathan asked, perhaps sensing that his invitation to Miriam had indeed been an interruption.

"She's... I don't know, perhaps. But she won't talk to me. She thinks I'm a child, they all do," Miriam replied.

Jonathan smiled. "I don't think you're a child, not at all. You're ready for your rumspringa, I don't know why your parents won't let you go already," he said.

Miriam laughed. "You know my parents," she said, glancing across the barn to where her *mamm* and *daed* were sitting with Bishop Beiler and his *fraa* Sarah. She loved them dearly, but they could be strict, and they had been adamant that Miriam was not allowed to go on her rumspringa until she was seventeen.

"And even then there'll be conditions," her *daed* had said, wagging his finger at her.

"Well, I think you're ready, but it's not my place to say," Jonathan replied.

"Look, I really should go after Leah. I don't know where she's gone, and I'm worried about her," Miriam said, unable to concentrate on anything but the thought of Leah and her odd words about Alma's adopted child.

"All right, I won't keep you. But see me tomorrow?" he asked.

Miriam nodded. "I'll see you tomorrow," she said, and setting aside her half-finished dish of shoofly pie, she smiled at him and slipped out of the barn, leaving the festivities behind.

It was almost dark now, the last rays of the sun setting over the cornfields, and with only one way leading in and out of the farm, she made her way through the gate and down the lane which led toward Faith's Creek. It was not long before she caught sight of Leah leaning on a gate that looked into a field. Increasing her stride, she hurried toward her. "Hey," she said.

Leah's head whipped around, a look of shock in her eyes. A hand flew to her chest and she took a breath. "What happened to Jonathan?"

"We had dessert, but I was worried about you," Miriam said.

"I'm all right, really, I am," she said.

Miriam could see that even though she had put on a brave face, that she wasn't. There was a sense of sadness that hung over her like a cloud. "I know you're not, and it's got something to do with a *boppli*."

The look on Leah's face told her she was right, but whether her friend was willing to reveal anything more was another question. Leah had always been a private person, reserved in her emotions, and even returning from her rumspringa had seemed to make no difference to her. She was still the shy and retiring type, a listener, rather than a talker, and never one to speak of her difficulties.

"I don't want to talk about it, Miriam, really, I don't. Can't you just accept that?" she said, her tone sounding sharp and unforgiving.

Miriam was somewhat taken aback. She only wanted to help her friend, and yet it seemed that whatever she said was wrong. "I only want to help. I'm worried about you. What you said to Sarah Beiler, it must have upset you something bad. You were crying back there. I don't want you to be sad. It's Alma's wedding day, you should be happy," she said, but Leah shook her head.

"I can't be happy, Miriam. Besides, Alma's wedding day is hardly the place to discuss my problems now, is it?" she said.

"But if you're sad, we should talk about it. We've been through enough to know when the other's hurting. I knew there was something more to this. You and Alma falling out and me being stuck in the middle. It was so awful, but I just want us all to get along together," she replied.

Miriam was tired of being treated as the youngster, never confided in, never trusted, never thought to have her own opinions. She could see Leah was hurting, and all she wanted to do was make it better.

"And we can, Miriam, but I don't want to talk about this, not with you, not with anyone, all right?" she said.

Miriam nodded. "All right, Leah, have it your way. But you can confide in me, you can trust me, I promise you," she said.

Leah gave her a weak smile in return. "I'm sorry. I don't mean to be like this with you, Miriam, I've just got a lot on my mind. You've always been a good friend to me, and I hope I've been a good friend to you, too, despite my failings."

Miriam put her arm around Leah and gave her a reas-suring squeeze. "You have, but my *mamm* always says "a problem shared is a problem halved," and I think that's true," Miriam replied.

"It is true, but sometimes we have to deal with our own problems in the best way we know how. It'll all work out in the end, I'm sure it will, and I promise I won't always be miserable. Shall I walk you home?" she said.

Miriam shook her head. "I left a half-eaten dish of shoofly pie behind with Jonathan. I should finish it. He'll be upset if I don't. Why don't you come with me?" she said.

Leah nodded. "All right, but no more talk about my problems, you hear me?" she said.

Miriam took her arm and nodded her agreement.

But as they walked back toward the barn, speaking of anything but their previous conversation, Miriam could sense the tension on Leah's every word and gesture. She knew her friend was in trouble, and despite Leah's protests, Miriam was determined to help.

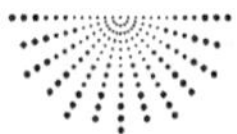

CHAPTER TWO

It was a few weeks after the wedding and Leah was sitting by the creek watching the waters meander by. It was one of her favorite places, and as a child, she would often go there to swim or sit reading on the banks. It was a place to be alone with her thoughts, and she had found a place where no one would see her, tucked beneath the branches of a great tree growing up at the water's edge. She had taken off her shoes and socks and was dangling her feet in the water, leaning back against one of the roots and daydreaming. She thought of her rumspringa, and all that had happened since the day she had left for Philadelphia on the Greyhound bus.

The memories were pleasant – some, at least – and she was soon lost in her thoughts, half asleep, drifting through pictures of what had been. Inevitably, she thought of Adam Garrett, a man she had met on her rumspringa, and with whom she had fallen in love. He had seemed the perfect man, tall and handsome, with tousled blond hair and a smile to match his charms. But it was his eyes that had so attracted her, deep green and thoughtful, eyes which even now she could picture gazing into hers. But all had not been as it seemed, and the pleasantness of those first encounters was tinged by the coldness of their parting days when Leah had returned to Faith's Creek with nothing but pain and hurt in her heart.

"What a fool I was," she said to herself, splashing her feet in the water, still with her eyes closed.

Now she yawned, tired from the days past, tired of Miriam asking her a dozen times if she was all right. Tired of everything. It was not long before she fell asleep, and her musings on her rumspringa turned into a reliving of the moment she had met Adam Garrett again. It had been quite by chance, the result of her journey to Philadelphia in search of Sawyer. Leah had gone there in the hope of repairing the damage she had done to her friendship with Alma, determined to reunite her and

Sawyer and see them happy in the end. Along the way, she had encountered Adam in a park where the two of them would often meet, and despite their mutual surprise, there was no doubting that both of them had been pleased to meet again...

As LEAH LAY on the bank she drifted back into the past.

Leah had just left Pickett's Coffee House on the corner of Page Street opposite Fairmount Park. It was one of her old haunts, and the owner – Lucy Pickett – had remembered her order, even after over a year of absence.

"Flat white, a dust of cocoa, and a shot of vanilla, isn't it?" she had said, and Leah had smiled, thanking the coffee shop owner, and buying a piece of blondie to go with her coffee.

It felt strange to be back in Philadelphia after returning home to Faith's Creek. But she was here for a reason, and that reason was Alma. After Sarah Beiler had attempted a reconciliation between them, Leah had felt a terrible sense of guilt for her judgment of her friend over the boppli she had adopted, and now she wanted to set things straight by finding Sawyer and reuniting them. Leah was certain she could persuade him of Alma's love for him and bring him back to Faith's Creek so that all of them might be reconciled.

It was a tall order, but one Leah had to attempt if she was to ever regain peace with herself and peace with Alma. She hated being at odds with her friend, and though she had her own reasons for finding what Alma had done a difficult thing to accept, it did not mean she had the right to judge her. Her mamm and daed had been surprised when she had announced her return to Philadelphia, but she had promised it would only be for a few weeks at most, and that when she returned, she would at last settle down and live the life expected of her. Now, she crossed her street and made her way into the park, taking her once familiar route around the East bank Reservoir, pausing to gaze across the grass toward Peters Island.

"Leah?" a voice to her side said, and she turned to find – to her astonishment – Adam Garrett smiling at her.

She blushed, recalling the last time they had been in one another's company and the curt parting which had occurred. But now, he smiled at her, and after all they had shared together, she could hardly dismiss him outright.

"Hello, Adam," she said, returning his smile.

"I didn't realize you were in Philadelphia... I mean... it's a big city, why would I, but I'm glad to meet you like this," he said.

"I'm here to... look for someone. It's complicated," she said.

He laughed. "Well, if you need any help, I'll happily look someone up for you. You still don't have a phone or anything, I suppose," he said.

She shook her head. "I find writing a letter far nicer than having some gadget pressed to my ear, or clasped in my hand," she said.

"I always liked how different you were. Say, why don't we sit down. Do you remember how often we used to come here? It was that bench right over there," he said, pointing across the park.

Leah could have chosen to decline his invitation. They had shared both joy and pain. Her memories of him were mixed, but she could not help but like him, and she was still attracted to him. There was something of fate, perhaps of His plan, in such a meeting, and she decided to allow it to continue on its course. Accepting his offer she walked with him across the grass to the bench they had spent so many happy hours sitting on together.

"I'm pleased to see you," she said, taking a sip of her coffee before splitting the piece of blondie in half and offering him the bigger piece.

"Thanks," he said, taking it and smiling.

"What have you been doing with yourself since... since I last saw you," she asked.

"Oh, just the usual, we've been supper busy at work, it's crazy at the moment," he said.

Adam worked in finance, he was an assistant to someone important, and he, in turn, had an assistant because he was important. It was a world far removed from the simple life Leah enjoyed in Faith's Creek, and now she had tasted both, she knew which one she preferred.

"You work hard, don't you," she said.

He sighed. "Too hard. There are days I'd love to swap places with you," he said.

She smiled. "You'd probably get bored soon enough."

It felt as though they were just picking up from where they last left off, as at ease in one another's company as they had ever been, and Leah could not help but be reminded of just how she had come to feel for him in the months they had spent together before her return to Faith's Creek. It felt strange to be sitting there, to recall the past, while the present felt so different. After several hours had gone by, she would gladly have remained with him forever. It was strange how easily her feelings were reignited. The past picked up, despite everything that had gone on between them, and the pain she had known at their separation replaced by a sense that everything might be all right if she would only allow it to be so.

"Then maybe you should come back here. Perhaps I might work less hard if you did," he said, laughing, as their eyes locked together.

Leah recalled the day he had kissed her on that very bench. "I don't know, I didn't think about that when I left. It was all so sudden, but meeting you and..." she said, as he reached out took her hand in his.

"Leah..." he began.

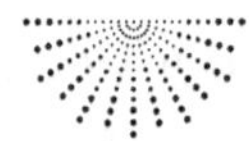

CHAPTER THREE

"Leah? Where are you, Leah?" a voice called out.

Leah sat up with a start, her feet splashing in the water, as she heard her *daed* – Matthew Fisher – calling out for her.

"Oh, I'm over here *Daed,* is it dinner time already?" she called out, scrambling to her feet and peering over the bank to find her *daed* standing on the path above with an exasperated look on his face.

"There you are, we've been waiting an hour for you. Your *mamm* told me to come down here and look for you. What happened, did you fall asleep?" he asked.

Leah nodded. "I couldn't help it, it's such a lovely day, and I was daydreaming and..." she said.

Matthew only shook his head and gave an exasperated sigh. "There's work to be done in the garden, Leah, and your *mamm's* got a list of chores as long as her arm. Come along now, let's get home," he said, beckoning for Leah to follow him.

Her parent's house lay just above the creek on the edge of the woods. It had a large garden in which her *daed* grew vegetables to sell at the market, and her *mamm* had a workshop at the back in which she would mend clothes and make new ones on commission. Leah helped both her parents at their work, though she was by no means a gardener, her *daed* often chastised her for pulling up plants instead of weeds.

"Leah, what time do you call this? It's past two, we've been ready to eat for an hour now. You told me you were going down to the creek at noon, not for the full day! Now sit down and eat, we've got work to do," Leah's *mamm*, Rebecca, said when she entered the house with her *daed* a short while later.

"I'm sorry, I didn't mean to be later. I was just sitting by the creek and then I fell asleep and..." she began, but Rebecca interrupted her.

"Daydreaming, Leah, you're always daydreaming. You need to live in the present a little more. There are chores to be done, and your *daed* needs help in the garden. Eat up, now," she said, pointing to the plate of food she had just placed on the table.

It was buttered noodles and chicken, one of Leah's favorites, but she could not find much appetite for it, pushing the food around the plate, and thinking back to the vivid dream which had just overtaken her. She had been back in Philadelphia, back with Adam, and all the thoughts and feelings which had accompanied that time had flooded back. She had gone to Philadelphia in search of Sawyer and with no intention of raking up the past, but the past had found her, and it had seemed that *Gott* had wanted her to meet Adam in the park that day, to rekindle what once had been, as painful as it was.

"What's wrong, Leah? You're acting so strangely today," Matthew said after Leah had taken only two bites of her food and pushed the rest aside.

"I don't want to talk about it," she replied.

Rebecca tutted. "Ever since you came back from Philadelphia you've been acting strangely, it's as though that city put a spell on you."

"I just want... I just want to be left alone," Leah replied, and rising to her feet, she fled from the house, tears running down her cheeks at the memories now flooding through her, and wondering if she had made the right decision or not...

OVER THE COMING DAYS, Leah avoided her parents as much as possible – she avoided everyone, in fact, preferring her own company for in it she could avoid the awkward questions which the likes of her *mamm, daed,* and Miriam would ask. She was miserable, bearing a burden which was almost too much for her, one which she knew would have dramatic consequences if the truth of it was known. Her chores now mounted, and she could summon little enthusiasm for anything, lost as she was in her own thoughts and fears.

"Oh, Leah, if you can't do it right, don't do it all," Rebecca told her after she had to unpick three of the four hems Leah had just finished sewing for her.

"I'm sorry, *Mamm,* I just can't concentrate on it," she said, tossing aside the sewing and sitting back on her chair with a sigh.

"Go and get some fresh air. Run down to the creek, take a walk through the cornfields, anything to bring you back with a mind set on work," Rebecca said, fixing her with an angry gaze.

"All right," Leah said, meekly rising from her place in the workroom and pulling on her shawl.

Outside, Leah was relieved to be in the fresh air, stifled as she had been by the atmosphere in the workroom. She made her way first down to the creek, pausing to sit by the waters. It was no good, her mind was still distracted by the thoughts which beset her – thoughts of the past, of Adam, and all that had happened in Philadelphia. She set off to speak to the one person she knew would understand.

Sarah Beiler opened the door with a smile on her face and ushered Leah inside. It had taken courage for Leah to come to the home of the Beiler's that day, but she had known that if she did not unburden herself fully to someone, then her troubles would overwhelm her.

"I thought you'd come," Sarah said, ushering her into the book-lined parlor and sitting her down in front of the hearth.

"You did?" Leah asked, and the bishop's *fraa* nodded.

She was an insightful woman, and Leah knew she could trust her, even with her deepest secrets. But despite this, she still felt nervous, carrying with her a revelation that would surely be shocking, even to one as kind and open as Sarah Beiler.

"You told me a lot of things at the wedding, but you didn't tell me everything. You were holding back on something, and when a person does that, then that something stays there. It keeps gnawing away, like a dog at a bone, wearing you down, and however hard you bury it, eventually it comes out," Sarah replied, sitting down opposite Leah and offering her tea from a freshly brewed pot.

"You're right. I didn't tell you everything," Leah said, taking a deep breath as she prepared to recount her story.

"Take your time. I know it won't be easy. You've nothing to worry about, it's better to share these things than keep them to yourself," Sarah said.

Leah nodded, pulling out a handkerchief and dabbing at her eyes. She felt foolish for crying, but the tears had been welling up for days, and now it was as though the floodgates were open and everything she had been holding back came pouring out.

"When I was on my rumspringa, I met a boy – a man – called Adam. He was so nice, so kind, and we got on really well. I was in love with him – I'm still in love with him," she said. Slowly she explained how she and Adam had enjoyed walks in the park and drinks at Pickett's Coffee House.

Sarah listened patiently, asking her questions every now and then, but mainly just listening, allowing Leah to tell her story.

"And that was the end of it? When you came back from your rumspringa, that is?" she said when Leah paused.

"That's the thing, I thought it would be. I convinced myself it would be, but it wasn't," she said, determined now to hold nothing back in her explanation.

"Did you see him again? Is that why you were upset at the wedding, you told me you knew how Alma felt, I didn't understand that part, I don't see you with a *boppli*," Sarah said, a puzzled expression on her face.

"Well, I don't have a *boppli*... not yet."

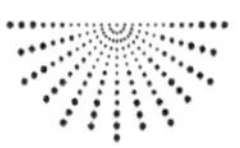

CHAPTER FOUR

"You see, when I went back to Philadelphia to look for Sawyer, I met Adam again – quite by chance. It was in the park where we used to take walks, and it was as though *Gott* had placed us both there at just the right time. I was amazed to see him and it was just like before, only... well, I couldn't help feeling sad at the way we'd parted before," Leah continued.

"Badly?" Sarah asked.

Leah nodded. "We'd had some heated words, he'd told me he had to take care of someone, someone that mattered. It was all very confusing until we met again, that is. Then he explained it," she replied.

The day they had met again had been something of a revelation to Leah, who had finally come to understand why Adam had been so cold and distant in those last days they had shared together. It was not because he did not love her, but because he was torn between duty and his heart.

"And what did he say?" Sarah asked.

Leah closed her eyes, knowing there could be no turning back. "I almost gave up everything for Adam – even Faith's Creek. I know that sounds terrible, but it's the truth. He meant everything to me, and I thought I meant everything to him. I was so upset when he froze me out, pushed me aside, and I never found out why until that day in the park. He told me it was all to do with a *boppli*," she said.

Sarah's eyes widened a little but she hid her shock well. "His *boppli*?" she asked.

Leah shook her head. "Not his *boppli*, no, the *boppli* of a friend, and now you know how close to home that is. It felt like he was telling Alma's story back to me. He had a friend, Jenny Warren, she'd had a hard life, her parents were abusive, her home life was a mess, she'd drifted from this to that, never finding her place. Adam took pity on her. He was kind like that, a magnet for people in need, and the two of them became friends – no more than that. Anyway, she fell pregnant by a man who wanted nothing to do with her, and her parents were no help. She had the *boppli* and then she asked Adam to take care of it. What else could he do but say yes? She wanted him to pose as the *boppli's daed*, and... Adam agreed. He couldn't tell me at the time – I don't know why, but he seemed to think it was better to just draw a line under our friendship and focus on the *boppli*. I suppose he was confused – it was just like Sawyer and Alma," Leah said, taking a sip of tea, as Sarah looked at her with a sympathetic gaze.

"And you find yourself unwittingly in the middle of it all. How awful, and shame on her parents for wanting nothing to do with the child. I feel so sorry for Jenny. No wonder Adam wanted to help," she said.

"He's such a good man, he'd do anything for anyone, that's why I felt so hurt when he froze me out. He was so cold, but now I know he was just trying to protect Jenny. He'd realized his mistake, but there was no way to contact me. I'd drawn a line under the relationship and come back to Faith's Creek hoping to make a fresh start," she said, taking another sip of tea.

It could only have been fate that brought them back together, and Leah was convinced she had been destined to meet Adam in the park that day. But what he had told her caused such a dilemma in her heart, one she had brooded on since returning, one she now needed to share.

"And what happened to the *boppli*?" Sarah asked.

"Well, that's just it, after all this, Jenny couldn't cope with being a *mamm*, even with Adam's help she found it hard, and she fled, leaving him and Elizabeth – that's what they called her – in Philadelphia. Adam was working all the hours *Gott* sent to keep her, and he's finding it so hard to be a lone *daed*. It broke my heart to hear it. I wanted to do something for him, to find some way of helping him," Leah replied, brushing a tear from her eye.

She had not yet met Elizabeth, but from what Adam had told her, the *boppli* was already growing up fast, and she needed a *mamm* – as well as a *daed* – to take care of her.

"I'm sure you can be a good support to him. You could write to him, or even meet him in Philadelphia sometimes. It's not that far on the Greyhound bus, only a few hours," Sarah said.

Leah shook her head. "There's more to it than that. Adam's worried – he's worried that Jenny's parents might swoop in at any moment and seek custody. They've threatened it already, and apparently, they know where he lives, where Elizabeth lives. He has her at daycare while he's at work, but it's just getting too much for him now. I wanted to help, and I told him I'd do anything I could for him and Elizabeth. He was grateful for that, and he asked me... well, he asked me if I'd help hide Elizabeth here in Amish country," she said.

Sarah's eyes grew wide with astonishment. "And what did you say?"

"I said I'd do it. I'm ready for a *boppli*, and I'll do anything I can to help Adam," she said, relieved to have finally unburdened herself.

She had hardly needed to think twice about her decision. Adam had told such a terrible tale that she could hardly refuse him, and she had felt an even stronger sense of *Gott* leading her along the right path. It was meant to be, the chance meeting in the park, the possibility of helping him, the hope of a child – all of it felt like *Gott's* will, and so Leah had willingly accepted.

The plan was simple enough. Leah would go back to Philadelphia a few weeks later and bring Elizabeth home to Faith's Creek. The small matter of what her parents – or anyone else for that matter – would say, seemed unimportant at the time. But since returning home with Sawyer, Leah had become ever more anxious about the prospect of what was to come. She had not yet summoned the courage to tell her parents and keeping her secret had seemed a hard task indeed, one which had now found expression in her confession to Sarah Beiler.

"And you're going to bring the *boppli* back soon?" Sarah asked, still looking at Leah's revelation.

"Next week, I've already booked the tickets on the Greyhound bus. I write to Adam each day, and he writes back. There's no time to lose, not if we're going to keep her safe. I'd have brought her back there and then, but I had Sawyer to find, and the time wasn't right," she replied.

"But are you certain about this, Leah? It's an enormous responsibility," Sarah said.

Leah nodded. She knew what a responsibility it was to take care of a child, but she owed it to Adam to help him. He had done so much for her in Philadelphia, and she had come to love him, as he had come to love her, too. Leah was determined to do all she could to help him, and whether or not her parents accepted it, soon there would be a new *boppli* in Faith's Creek...

CHAPTER FIVE

"I'm so excited about going to Philadelphia, I still can't believe my parents allowed it. I suppose I'm going with you, and they trust you, and know you'll not do anything foolish," Miriam said, as she and Leah sat looking out of the window of the Greyhound bus.

It was the day that Adam would hand Elizabeth to Leah, and she had brought Miriam with her to offer moral support, even though Miriam had no idea of her intention in doing so. Miriam thought they were having a day trip, a chance to look around the city before her own rumspringa the following year, and she could not be more excited.

"We'll have a nice day. You deserve a little break from Faith's Creek," Leah said, trying to disguise, as best she could, her growing nerves at the prospect of returning home with Elizabeth.

She had not found the right words to explain to her parents what was to happen, nor had she revealed the secret to anyone other than Sarah Beiler. Sarah had done much to support her in the days following the dramatic revelation. The bishop's *fraa* had found clothes for Elizabeth, and other items necessary for the proper care of a *boppli*. She had passed them discreetly to Leah, who had hidden them in her bedroom in preparation. In her mind, all would be well, though there was still much left in question, and much left to chance.

"I want to see everything. Can we have one of those hot chocolates you talked about? With the marshmallows and whipped cream on top?" Miriam asked.

Leah laughed. "You can have two, though I doubt you'll manage one," she said.

Miriam's face lit up. "Oh, I can't wait," she said, pressing her nose to the glass as Leah took a deep breath to steady her nerves.

Upon their arrival in Philadelphia, they thanked the bus driver and made their way through the bus terminal and out onto the street. It was busy, and Miriam appeared quite overwhelmed by the hustle and bustle.

"This way, we'll go to the park first," Leah said, glancing at a clock on a nearby church that had just struck midday.

She was due to meet Adam at one o'clock, and they called into Pickett's Coffee House first, where Leah allowed Miriam to choose anything she wanted. Miriam was so excited she could barely contain herself, and she kept asking all manner of questions as they walked together into Fairmount Park. Leah's nerves were growing more fraught by the moment.

"I've never been in such a big place before. Do all these people really live here? What else is there to see? Where did you live? Didn't you want to stay here forever?" Miriam exclaimed, gazing around her in awe.

"You get used to it, I suppose," she said, gazing around her absent-mindedly.

She was listening out for the sound of the clock chimes, Adam had agreed to wait for her on the bench they usually sat on, and she glanced across toward Peters Island, seeing him there, holding Elizabeth in his arms.

"What's that over there? It looks like a castle," Miriam exclaimed, pointing to a folly known as the cliffs, which was now more famous for its graffiti.

"Why don't you go and look. I'll be over here. We might get an ice cream soon," Leah said.

Miriam smiled and nodded. Leah watched until she was out of sight before hurrying over to the bench, where Adam rose to greet her.

"You made it," he said, as Elizabeth looked up from his arms and smiled at Leah, whose heart melted at the sight.

"Oh... she's beautiful, Adam. Look at her," she exclaimed.

Adam held her out for Leah to take. "She's been waiting to meet you," Adam said, though there was a note of sadness in his voice, and Leah knew how difficult it would be for him to give Elizabeth up.

"This is the right thing for her, she'll be safe in Faith's Creek until all this blows over. Jenny's parents don't really want her, they want to cause trouble, just like they did for their own daughter. I'll look after her, and you can come and see her whenever you want, every week-end," Leah said, as Elizabeth wriggled in her arms.

"She has a bottle about this time, I've packed all her things here, and if she doesn't sleep at night, her teddy bear's in there, she likes to hold it, and, another thing..." he said, but Leah shushed him.

"It'll be all right, it's only for a few weeks, we'll be all right," she said, hoisting Elizabeth up into a sitting position so that Adam could see her properly.

"My beautiful little angel, don't forget how much I love you," he said, kissing her gently on the forehead. "Were your parents all right about all this?"

Leah smiled, not wishing to tell him the truth about how few people knew of Elizabeth's imminent arrival.

"Oh... yes, they can't wait to meet her," she said.

Adam nodded and let out a sigh of relief. "All right, well, I'd better go. If I stay any longer, I'll want her back. I know you'll take good care of her, Leah," he said, and he kissed her on the cheek as he did so.

The kiss brought back memories of other kisses, other moments they had shared, some on that very bench in front of them. Leah found herself longing for those moments again, for the things left behind, the things she had thought confined to the past and now rediscovered.

"Say goodbye to your *daed*, Elizabeth. He'll see you soon, I promise," she said.

Adam put his finger into Elizabeth's hand, as she gurgled up at him with a smile. "Goodbye, little angel," he whispered, and brushing a tear from his eyes, he hurried off across the park, leaving Leah and Elizabeth alone.

To find herself responsible for a *boppli* was a daunting thought, one which Elizabeth had not been entirely prepared for. She had seen Alma with Samuel often enough, watched her take care of him – feed him, bathe him, dress, and rock him to sleep, and she had held Samuel, too, but this was quite different. She was responsible, and no one else was there to help. She watched as Adam disappeared from view, and then looked down at Elizabeth, who gazed up at her with a look of gurgling adoration.

"Well, it's just you and me now," she whispered, cradling Elizabeth in her arms.

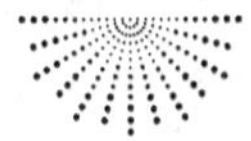

CHAPTER SIX

To say that seeing Leah cradling a *boppli* in her arms was a surprise would be an understatement. Miriam had got slightly lost in the park, delighting in the freedom of her day in Philadelphia, and had stopped at an ice cream cart to buy two ice pops and a bottle of Coca-Cola. She almost dropped them at the sight of Leah sitting there with a *boppli* in her arms. For a moment, she wondered if she had returned to the right place. But there could be no mistaking Leah's appearance! Miriam hurried over to her, astonished at the sight.

"What's this?" she asked, staring at Leah in wide-eyed astonishment, as the *boppli* now began to wriggle and cry.

"You'd better sit down. I've got a lot to tell you," Leah replied.

The ice pops were melting fast, but Miriam could only think of the extraordinary sight before her, desperate to hear the explanation which Leah surely owed her.

"I'd say you do. Where did it... he?" she asked, and Leah shook her head.

"She, and she's not mine before you ask. I'm just... taking care of her for someone," Leah replied.

"Taking care of her? Wait, you need to explain this from the start. Is this to do with Alma? Is this why you got so upset?" she asked.

Leah nodded. "That's right, but it's a long story," she replied.

"We've got time," Miriam said, opening the bottle of Coca-Cola and taking a long draught.

She listened in astonishment as Leah explained how she had come to Philadelphia and met a man named Adam Garrett. A man who would ultimately find himself charged with the care of a *boppli*, abandoned by its *mamm* and with no *daed* to want it. The *boppli* – Elizabeth – was in danger of being taken by her grandparents, abusive parents who caused such misery to poor Jenny Warren, the *mamm* of the child. Leah explained Adam had trusted her with the care of the child until it was safe for her to return to Philadelphia.

"And we'll keep her hidden, I know we will," Leah said, stating the fact as though it were the most obvious thing in the world.

"So, you're going to take a *boppli* that isn't yours back to Faith's Creek and hide it," Miriam said, thinking this sounded completely absurd.

"Exactly," Leah replied.

"And your *mamm* and *daed*? They know about this?" Miriam asked.

Leah shook her head. "They will – once we arrive back in Faith's Creek," she said.

Miriam's eyes went wide in disbelief. "You haven't told them?"

Leah shook her head. "I didn't find the right moment, that's all. Sarah Beiler knows. That was what we were talking about that night at the wedding. Well, part of it, at least. I told her everything, she's supportive and she'll talk to my parents if necessary," she said.

Miriam shook her head, hardly able to comprehend the enormity of what was being said.

Of the three friends: Miriam, Alma, and Leah, it was Leah who had always been the sensible one. The one to find fault with Miriam's wild ideas, who reined her in when excitement got the better of her. But here was Leah, seemingly entirely devoid of reason and talking as though it were the most natural thing in the world to take a boppli that was not hers back home to a family that was not expecting it and believing that the whole thing would work out perfectly.

"But it all seems... so incredible," Miriam said.

"Sometimes we do things that don't quite make sense. But I know it's the right thing. I want to help Adam, and Elizabeth doesn't deserve to go to those awful people. Whatever faults her *mamm* might have, she's just an innocent *boppli*. If we can give her the best start in life, then that's all that matters," Leah replied.

"But what will people say? Back in Faith's Creek, I mean. You can't just turn up with a *boppli* and expect everyone to accept it," Miriam said, imagining what her own parents would say if she were to do such a thing.

"They accepted Alma's *boppli*, didn't they? Sarah Beiler says it'll be all right. And it's not forever. I'm just looking after her, that's all," Leah said, gazing down lovingly at Elizabeth, who now began to cry.

"I think she needs feeding," Miriam said, certain that Leah was out of her mind.

"Come on, we'd better get back to the bus terminal. We don't want to miss the Greyhound home," Leah said, entirely oblivious to the astonishing situation she had created.

Reluctantly, Miriam followed her, all thoughts of a happy day in Philadelphia gone, replaced with a sense of foreboding as to what was now to come. She thought of Leah's parents, of Alma and the rest of the community. Would they really accept another *boppli* blown in from Philadelphia? Only time would tell, and as they boarded the Greyhound bus that afternoon, Miriam was certain that Leah's hopes for a happy ending were merely wishful thinking...

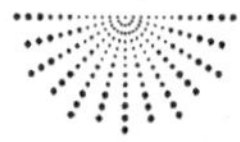

CHAPTER SEVEN

*L*eah had not been surprised at Miriam's reaction – it was hardly an everyday occurrence to find your closest friend cradling a *boppli* when you had only gone for ice cream and soda. But on the journey back to Faith's Creek, her earlier disbelief seemed to change to tacit acceptance. By the time they stepped off the bus, she was holding Elizabeth in her arms and making cooing noises at her.

"You've still got to convince your parents," Miriam said, as they walked slowly along the lane which led through the cornfields toward Faith's Creek.

"They'll be surprised. I know they will. Who wouldn't be? But when they hear the story... well, they can't say no, can they?" Leah asked.

She was rather relying on the goodwill of those around her to accept Elizabeth into their hearts. She was hardly a souvenir of Philadelphia, the sort of thing brought back from a day trip north to the city of brotherly love. This was life-changing, not only for Leah but for her parents, too. Still, she reminded herself that it was not meant to be forever and that when the situation with Jenny's parents was resolved, Adam would come to bring his daughter home.

"But what about you? Will you cope with a *boppli* on your own? It's such a big responsibility, isn't it? Alma has Sawyer there, and they manage well together, but you'll have no one but yourself," Miriam said, as they came in sight of Leah's parent's house.

"I've always wanted a *boppli*. I know that sounds foolish – it should be a husband first and then a *boppli*… but the thought of taking care of something so precious. It's just so special," Leah said, gazing down at Elizabeth, whom Miriam had passed back to her, and whom she now held in her arms.

At first, the responsibility for a child had seemed daunting to say the least, but Leah had vowed to herself that with love, anything was possible. She would do her best by Elizabeth, and whilst there would be mistakes along the way, Leah knew that what mattered was for the *boppli* to be loved and taken care of.

"Do you want me to come in with you?" Miriam asked as they came to the garden gate.

"Would you mind?" Leah asked, knowing her *mamm* and *daed* could not fly into quite such a rage if Miriam was there, too.

"Of course, I wouldn't mind," Miriam said, smiling at Leah, "I've got a *boppli* sister to take care of now, not to mention a *boppli* brother, too," and she laughed.

Leah had always thought of Alma and Miriam as sisters, and with the arrival of the two *bopplis*, it felt like their families were growing. She could not wait to introduce Elizabeth to Samuel and hoped the two children would play together, and grow together as friends. Leah knew she would only have a short time with Elizabeth, but she wanted to make the most of that time. Taking a deep breath, she opened the garden gate, knowing that life would never be the same again...

* * *

THERE WAS something of a delayed reaction on Rebecca's face at the sight of her daughter carrying a *boppli*.

The house was filled with the sweet aroma of baking, and Matthew was sitting at the table in the parlor with his back turned to the door, reading his Bible.

"Oh, there you both are. Did you have a nice day? You must have been so excited to go to Philadelphia, Miriam, and... oh, my!" Rebecca exclaimed, almost dropping a dish of noodles as she spoke.

Matthew turned to see what all the fuss was about, and his eyes grew wide with astonishment at the sight before him.

"*Mamm, Daed*, this is Elizabeth," Leah said, holding out the *boppli*, as her *mamm* and *daed* looked at one another in astonishment.

"But... what? She's not... yours, is she?" Rebecca demanded.

Leah shook her head. "Will you sit down, *Mamm*? I know I've got a lot of explaining to do," she said, as Rebecca clutched at the tabletop to steady herself from the shock.

"But if she's not yours then... whose is she?" Matthew asked.

Leah took a seat at the far end of the table, still cradling Elizabeth in her arms. "She not mine, she's..." she began, but Rebecca interrupted her again.

"Miriam! What will your parents say?" she exclaimed.

Miriam shook her head. "Oh, I'm as surprised as you are," she said.

Leah held up her hand and explained all that had taken place in Philadelphia and the chain of events that had led to this most surprising arrival.

When she had finished her explanation, her *mamm* and *daed* looked at one another, and Rebecca shook her head and sighed.

"Why didn't you tell us? You can't just turn up with a *boppli* and expect us to take it in as our own. Do you know what kind of responsibility this is? She's not your child, Leah. You can't just take her and hide her away. If she was in danger, you should have taken her to the proper authorities, not whisked her away to Faith's Creek. What were you thinking?"

"I... I don't know, but I couldn't bear to see her suffer at the hands of those awful people. She doesn't deserve that. It's only for a while – until Adam can find a safe place for them both to live. He'll come and fetch her then. But you can't send her back, *Mamm*, please. Oh... *Daed*, tell her, tell her Elizabeth can stay," Leah replied, turning imploringly to her *daed*, who shook his head and sighed.

Somehow, Leah had believed her *mamm* and *daed* would take kindly to Elizabeth, that they would welcome her with open arms, but the opposite seemed to be the case, and now she looked desperately at them both, tears welling up in her eyes at the realization of what she had done.

"I agree with your *mamm*, Leah. It was a reckless thing to do. You can't just take a *boppli* in like this. There are rules over such things, and what if this Jenny Warren comes looking for her daughter? You've no legal right to take care of her, whatever the circumstances might be. We can't just hide a *boppli* here until things blow over back in Philadelphia," he said.

"I should be going," Miriam said, rising to her feet and looking embarrassed at being caught in the crossfire between Leah and her parents.

"Oh, you don't have to," Leah said, wishing her friend would stay to offer moral support.

"I'll call on you tomorrow," Miriam said, and she put her hand gently on Elizabeth's forehead and leaned down to kiss her.

"And what's going to happen now? Can you take her back? Did anyone see you getting off the Greyhound bus?" Rebecca asked.

Leah shook her head. "I promised Adam," she said.

Both her parents gave exasperated cries.

"So, we're stuck with a boppli now, are we, and..." Matthew began, just as a knock came at the door.

"Quickly, hide in the parlor," Rebecca said.

Leah rose to her feet, glancing anxiously toward the door as Miriam made her excuses to leave.

In the parlor, Elizabeth began to cry, and Leah held her close, shushing her lest she screams. But the voice which came from the kitchen brought her a sigh of relief, and she stepped back out from the parlor to find Sarah Beiler greeting her parents.

"Oh, there you are, Leah. I thought you'd be back about this time," Sarah said.

Leah's parents looked at one another again in disbelief.

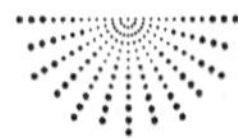

CHAPTER EIGHT

"*D*id you know about this?" Matthew asked, his tone only just maintaining an air of respect and his eyes and color even less so.

"I knew about it, Matthew, that's right. Leah confided in me, and I've been helping her to prepare. I knew this would all come as a shock to you both, and that's why I came round this afternoon – we can talk about it... if you like," she said.

Leah stepped forward with Elizabeth in her arms. "You see, I wasn't entirely foolish," she said, addressing her parents.

"But... you can't possibly think this is a good idea?" Matthew said.

Sarah smiled and reached out and took Elizabeth in her arms. "To take a child from danger and give it a decent home? To love and care for it, as I'm certain Leah will? Oh, I think it's a great idea," she replied, rocking Elizabeth back and forth and shushing her.

"But the responsibility, it's too much," Rebecca said.

Sarah shook her head. "She's ready for it. Besides, if it's *Gott's* will that this happens, then who are we to argue with that?" she asked.

It was that knowledge that had convinced Leah of the rightness of what she was doing. Fate had brought her and Adam together, and fate had reunited them by chance. She was convinced – and in her conversations with Sarah Beiler had become more so – that this was what *Gott* wanted for her: to be a loving *mamm* to Elizabeth for just so long as she needed her. To keep the precious bundle safe and loved while things were sorted out for her.

"Do you really think so?" Rebecca asked, and a change seemed to come over her as she looked down at Elizabeth and smiled.

"So often, it's the innocent child who's hurt by the actions of those around it," Sarah said. "Elizabeth knows nothing of all that has happened. All she needs is love, and I'm certain Leah will give that to her in abundance. Feel blessed and pray on this and you too will see that this is the right path. I have heard all about Elizabeth's grandparents and Adam has a letter from the *boppli's mamm* stating her wishes. This is for the best."

Leah was grateful to Sarah for her words. If anyone could convince her *mamm* and *daed* that what she was doing was right, then it was Bishop Beiler's *fraa*. She was a voice of reason and one which her parents would listen to. Miriam had left now, and Sarah passed Elizabeth back to Leah, who cradled her in her arms and smiled.

"You didn't tell us about the letter," Matthew said.

"That does make it easier," Rebecca agreed.

"I only want to do what's right by Elizabeth, and by Adam, too. He needed help, and I was able to give it to him," Leah said, looking up at both her parents.

They shared a glance and gradually seemed to relax, eventually, they nodded.

"Well... I suppose it would only be for a short time, and if it's really for the best – for the good of Elizabeth," Rebecca said.

"But there are still so many things we don't know... and what about this man, Adam? Were you in love with him? What happened between you?" Matthew asked.

Leah blushed. "When we first parted I thought he was in love with Jenny Warren, we had some cross words, it wasn't what it seemed, though, really, it wasn't," she said, and her *daed* nodded.

"There's more to this than you're telling us, Leah, I don't think..." he began, but it was her *mamm* who interrupted now.

"Matthew, this is *Gott's* will, and we're part of that. Maybe we need to have a little more faith, don't you think?" she asked, and Matthew sighed reluctantly.

"I don't want to be kept up at all hours of the night by a screaming *boppli*, I've done that once. I thought my parenting days were over," he said, and Leah smiled.

"Does that mean she can stay?" she asked, glancing at Sarah, who nodded.

"For now, yes, but I'm not happy about it," Matthew said.

Leah laughed, held Elizabeth up in her arms as the *boppli* gave a gurgling exclamation.

"Did you hear that? Welcome home," she said.

"Well, I think I'd better be going. I'll bring some more things around for Elizabeth tomorrow," Sarah said, rising from the table and bidding Leah's parents good day.

"*Denke*, Sarah," Rebecca said, but the bishop's *fraa* shook her head.

"You don't need to thank me. Just be grateful you've raised a daughter with such a great capacity for love," she said.

With that, she departed, leaving Leah and her parents to care for a new *boppli*, a day which none of them would ever forget...

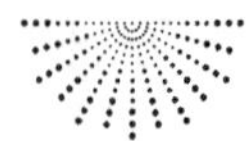

CHAPTER NINE

The coming weeks passed in what Leah felt was perfect bliss. She was a natural, born to be a *mamm*, or so it seemed. She delighted in every task – however menial – and in caring for Elizabeth, she gained a sense of purpose she had never felt before. Here was a life that needed her, and which she needed, too. She loved Elizabeth with all her heart and she was so proud to call the little girl her own.

There had been some surprise in Faith's Creek at the appearance of Leah Fisher with a *boppli*, and obviously, questions were asked. But it was soon known that she, like Alma, had adopted a baby from Philadelphia, a child in need of love and care in a community such as Faith's Creek and there could be no scandal in that.

"I think Elizabeth needs feeding, Leah," Rebecca said, as Elizabeth rolled on her back on the play mat in the parlor, making gurgling noises.

"Really, Mamm! I only gave her a bottle an hour ago," Leah replied.

"But she's growing so fast. Look at her, isn't she adorable?" Rebecca replied, leaning down to tickle Elizabeth's chin so that she laughed.

"I'll take her upstairs," Leah said, lifting Elizabeth into her arms and kissing her on the forehead, "my, you've grown so much."

Leah's parents had accepted Elizabeth, though her *daed* was still somewhat grudging in his affections. But even he had come to see the sense in giving a home to a child in need and had even been known to sit Elizabeth on his knee and play with her.

Rebecca treated Elizabeth as though she were the grandchild she had always longed for. Together, she and Leah had taken care of her, so that there could be no doubting that Faith's Creek was the best place possible for the child who's adopted *daed* remained in Philadelphia.

Leah had written to Adam every week since her return home, telling him everything about Elizabeth and always reiterating her invitation for him to come and join them.

But it was not only as Elizabeth's *daed* that she wished Adam to come to them, but also as the man she was still in love with. Despite everything that had passed between them, Leah could not change how she felt about him. She loved him, and she wished for nothing else but for the three of them to be a family. Leah did not like to think about the day when she might have to give Elizabeth up, concentrating instead on the happy moments they had together, and the memories they could make.

"Come on now, let's sit down and give you a bottle," she said, settling herself in a rocking chair by the window and cradling Elizabeth in her arms.

She thought of Adam, wondering if he was thinking of them, too. She missed him terribly, and she was sure Elizabeth did, too. It must have seemed strange to her to be taken away from that familiar face. Leah hoped it would not be too long before they were all reunited. It was not easy being a *mamm* to Elizabeth, but Leah was doing her best, and she was certain the child was happy. The whole thing had been a terrible tragedy, and Elizabeth was the innocent party in it all, deserving of love and care – the love which Leah was determined to give her.

"Leah, come down here," Rebecca called out, "Alma's here, and she's brought Samuel with her, too"

Leah smiled. She had not seen Alma for a week or so and was glad of a visit from her friend. Miriam had called around often, offering to help with Elizabeth, and bringing with her all sorts of toys and gifts. Leah was lucky to have such close friends, and now she rose from the rocking chair with Elizabeth in her arms and made her way down to the parlor where Alma was waiting for her. Samuel seemed to be growing bigger by the day, and the two women embraced as the *bopplis* looked at one another curiously.

"Do you think they talk to one another? Or understand one another?" Alma asked as they sat down by the hearth, each holding their charge in their arms.

"I suppose they must, or perhaps they just look at one another and wonder what on earth's going on," Leah replied, laughing and shaking her head.

"How are you finding it? Being a *mamm*, I mean?" Alma asked.

"I love every minute of it. It's the most wonderful thing in the world. I couldn't think of anything that would make me happier," Leah replied.

Alma smiled, a serene smile filled with peace. "I know just how you feel. When I first held Samuel, I was convinced I'd never be a good *mamm*, but you get used to it, it sort of just happens, doesn't it?" she said.

Leah nodded. "I've made some mistakes, but that's fine, she's happy, but I know she misses her *daed,*" Leah replied.

She had told Alma the full story of Adam and the events in Philadelphia, though she had kept back the full extent of her feelings for him. Her thoughts on the matter were confused, and though she knew she loved him, she was uncertain how deep his feelings for her ran in return. He had spoken of love, he had shown it by his actions, but the situation was so complicated that Leah did not want to confuse matters further by racing ahead – she would let Adam make the first move.

"Will Adam come and see her?" Alma asked.

"I hope so," she replied, for she had invited him a dozen times in every one of her letters to him over the previous few weeks.

"Leah, there's something I wanted to tell you – about Adam, that is," Alma said, and Leah looked at her with a puzzled expression.

She did not know that Alma knew anything of Adam. The two had never met – unless their paths had crossed by chance in Philadelphia.

"About Adam? What do you know about him?" Leah asked.

"It's Sawyer. He saw you and Adam speaking in Philadelphia – he was there to collect some things from his old place, and he saw the two of you in the park," she said.

"He was spying on us?" Leah asked, astonished at the thought of her friend's husband behaving in such a way.

"No, it was just by chance – like so much of all this is by chance. But he was there again this past week, and he saw Adam again, and this time he spoke to him and..." Alma replied, but Leah interrupted her.

"He saw him? But Adam's supposed to have disappeared, he's not supposed to be anywhere near Philadelphia, not in public, at least. Jenny's parents are looking for him. That's why I took Elizabeth – to make it easier for him to hide," she said.

Adam had made no mention of meeting Sawyer, and in his letters, he had assured Leah he was lying low, keeping out of the way and waiting for the trouble to pass. This meeting felt like a betrayal, and Leah wondered how Adam could have behaved in such a way when he had Elizabeth and her to think of.

"I don't know the details. Sawyer didn't, either. I don't know why Adam wasn't hiding. All I know is that they met – it was a bar or something. Sawyer saw Adam, and the two got talking. He told him he recognized him and that was that. They parted ways and Sawyer told me about it when he got home. I didn't realize he had to hide," Alma replied.

"For Elizabeth's sake, he has to. We can't keep her safe if he doesn't. If they find him, there's no telling what they might do to him, and then they'll come looking for Elizabeth," Leah said, glancing fearfully at the door as though she expected Jenny Warren's parents to come bursting through at any moment and demand the return of Elizabeth.

"I'm sure it'll be all right. Is there something else? More going on?" she asked.

Leah shook her head.

She had been surprised at the force of her feelings, surprised by the sense of panic which had risen inside her at the thought of Adam being found. She did not want to admit how much she loved him, how much she longed for him to come to Faith's Creek, and how she desired they might be a family together at last.

"Nothing, no, I was just surprised, that's all. I didn't think Sawyer knew Adam," she replied.

Alma smiled. "He doesn't, not really, but it's a small world, and I suppose they just recognized one another and got talking," Alma replied.

Leah nodded. She did not want to make an issue of the encounter, though it still seemed strange to think it was a mere coincidence. She did not like the thought of Sawyer watching her and Adam in the park, but if the facts were simple enough, she was willing to push her worries aside. Adam would keep himself safe, of that, she was certain.

"And Samuel's growing up so fast, isn't he?" Leah said, changing the subject abruptly.

"He gets bigger by the day, he's starting to look like a proper little boy now," she said, smiling down at her son, who was asleep in her arms.

"And when does Samuel get a little brother or sister?" Leah asked, and Alma blushed and laughed.

"Oh... I don't think we're quite ready for that yet. Perhaps in a few years," she replied.

"A few years? Oh, you can't wait that long," Leah exclaimed.

"But what about you? Aren't you worried you'll never find a husband with a *boppli* in tow? You don't know how long Elizabeth's going to be here, and there aren't many men who would take on a *boppli* like that, not with so many questions attached," Alma replied.

Her words were no doubt meant kindly, but they struck a sour note with Leah, who was not concerned with such questions. She had no interest in seeking a man – as far she was concerned, Adam was the man for her, and it was only a matter of time before the two of them might be together.

"I don't mind," she said, her tone sounding sharp.

Alma nodded. "All right, we just want you to be happy," she replied.

Leah knew from the word "we," that Alma had been talking to Miriam. They did that sometimes, as did Miriam and Leah, and Miriam and Alma – talk about the other behind their backs. It was never malicious, done only out of concern, but now, Leah had heard enough.

"I'm perfectly all right," she said.

Alma nodded, glancing at the clock on the mantelpiece and letting out an exclamation. "Is that the time? I should be going," she said, rising to her feet just as Samuel promptly woke up and began to cry.

There was much shushing, and Elizabeth too awoke, so that the parlor was filled with the cries of the two babies. Rebecca came in from the kitchen to see what all the commotion was about.

"They'll wake the dead," she cried.

"Alma was just going," Leah replied, and she nodded to Alma, who now made her way out onto the porch, calling out a goodbye as she went, desperately trying to quiet the screaming Samuel.

With Elizabeth now calm, Leah sat back down in a chair next to the hearth and sighed. It was strange to think of Sawyer and Adam together, and she wondered what they had talked about and when Adam would finally make the journey to Faith's Creek.

"I hope we see your *daed* soon," she said, smiling down at Elizabeth, who gazed back up at her with wide, loving eyes, the picture of innocence in a very complicated world.

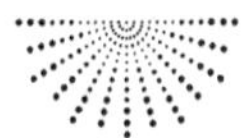

nother month went by, and Leah had only one letter from Adam in that time, sent from a forwarding address she had never heard of before. It contained little by way of news, assuring her merely of his affections for Elizabeth and that he would see them both very soon. It puzzled her to think he should be making so little effort toward the daughter he professed to love, but Leah was so busy taking care of Elizabeth that she had little time to think to the contrary.

It was fortunate that her parents had now accepted Elizabeth into their lives, and even her *daed* admitted he rather liked being a *grossdaddi* after all. Both her parents doted on Elizabeth, and from time to time, they would allow Leah to take a walk by herself or visit Miriam or

Alma alone. Both her friends were supportive, and Leah was in no doubt that she had made the right decision in bringing Elizabeth home to Faith's Creek.

"Why don't you take a walk by the creek or out over the cornfields. We'll be all right with Elizabeth, she's settled now," Rebecca said.

It was a bright, sunny afternoon, and just the sort of day for a walk. Leah smiled and nodded, kissing Elizabeth on the forehead before putting on a shawl and straightening her kapp.

"I won't be long," she said, and Matthew smiled as he cooed at Elizabeth.

"Take as long as you want, we'll be fine with her," he said.

Leah nodded.

A change had certainly come over both her parents since Elizabeth's arrival – a change for the better. And now it seemed odd to think of life without Elizabeth. The longer she remained in Faith's Creek, the harder Leah knew it would be to let her go. She was as much a part of the family as any of them and loved by them all.

Leah took the path from the bottom of the garden down toward the creek, intending to sit in her favorite spot and watch the waters go by. It was a hot day, and she imagined the feel of the water on her toes, pleased to have a moment of peace amidst the busy life she had created for herself. Taking care of a *boppli* was hard work, and while Leah delighted in it, she was glad of even the briefest respite.

The water was cool and inviting, and Leah dangled her feet from the edge of the bank, splashing the water, and watching the ripples fade out across the surface. She closed her eyes and began to daydream, imagining herself back in Philadelphia with Adam.

They would sit in the park on days like this, drinking lemonade and lying on their back to watch the clouds drift slowly by. They had been such blissful days, filled with happiness, and imagining herself back there was a way of reconnecting with what seemed to have been lost. She missed Adam terribly, and though the thought of him was painful, she could not help but think of him, too.

She had found herself more and more preoccupied with Adam in recent days, wondering where he might be and what he might be doing. It was the sense of the unknown she found hardest to accept – that Adam could be anywhere, and she would not know. She did not want Elizabeth to grow up without her *daed*, and she was certain Adam did not want that, either. His continued absence was all the stranger for this, for Leah knew how much it had pained him to give Elizabeth up into her care. As she sat on the bank, she prayed for Adam, asking *Gott* to keep him safe and bring him home to them when the time was right. Her prayer was disturbed by the crack of a twig behind her, and she turned with a start to peer through the trees.

"Hello?" she called out, peering into the undergrowth.

There had definitely been someone there, someone lurking in the shadows, and she rose to her feet and called out a second time, again hearing the sound of cracking twigs, as footsteps came closer.

"Leah?" a voice called out, and to her horror she saw Adam, stumbling out from the shadows, his face bruised, his clothes torn, his appearance haggard.

He was such a contrast to the man she knew, and whom she had last seen striding across the park in Philadelphia.

"Adam," she gasped, rushing forward and throwing her arms around him.

He looked as though he had slept the night in the forest, his hair disheveled and unkempt, his eyes puffy and his face smeared with dirt.

"What happened to you? How did you get here?" she asked, her mind filled with questions.

He shook his head and began mumbling something about the Greyhound bus and Jenny's parents. He was making no sense, and she took him by the hand and led him toward the creek, making him sit down on a tree stump at the water's edge and catch his breath.

"I had to come, I had to see you," he exclaimed and she nodded.

"And I'm glad you're here, but what happened? You look a terrible mess," she said, taking his hands in hers and kneeling in front of him.

"It's all been a terrible mess," he said, sighing, and hanging his head as though in shame.

"Tell me what's happened. I know you've written a few times, but it always felt you were holding something back. What's been going on?" she asked, certain now that there was far more to be revealed than his letters had done.

"Is Elizabeth all right?" he gasped, and Leah nodded.

"She's with my parents, but it's you I'm concerned for. You look terrible," she said.

It was true, he did. Back in Philadelphia, Adam was always smartly turned out. It had been one of the many things which had attracted her to him when they had first met. It had been at a jazz bar in the first few days of her rumspringa. Now he looked a mess, and there was bruising on his face and neck, the result, it appeared, of an altercation.

"A lot's happened since I saw you last," he began, catching his breath and slowing his words.

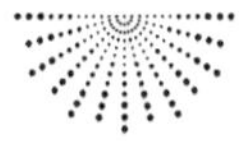

CHAPTER ELEVEN

"You need those injuries seeing to," Leah said.

Slowly, he shook his head. "Let me tell the story first."

She nodded, waiting until he was ready to speak again.

"I was going to hide from Jenny's parents. To lie low until I could slip away and find somewhere safe for Elizabeth and me to live. But it wasn't to be, my apartment was robbed – I don't know who by – but they took all the money I'd saved up and I was left with nothing. I had to keep working, saving as much as I could. It was all such a mess," he said.

Leah squeezed his hand, feeling overwhelming

sympathy for him in his plight – a plight she shared in, too.

"But you're safe now, aren't you? Who did this to you? The robbers?" she asked.

He shook his head. "No, Jenny's dad. He found out where I lived – just like we hoped to avoid. I got a nasty beating from him, and the threat of another if I went to the cops. I didn't know what to do, or where to go, so I came here on the first ticket I could find. I know it's not ideal, and I dread to think about what your parents will say. I just couldn't stop thinking of Elizabeth – I wanted to see her so badly, and I wanted to see you, too," he said, giving her a weak smile.

Despite his bruises and muddied face, it was the same familiar smile she had known in Philadelphia, and Leah threw her arms around him as tears rolled down her cheeks.

"Don't worry, you're safe now, they'll not find you here. Elizabeth's safe. You should see her. She's so happy. It's wonderful to see you, but I know she misses you. You can see it in her eyes – she wonders where that kind man is," Leah said.

Adam nodded. "I think about her all the time. I wonder what she's doing, if she's happy – everything," he said.

"Come on, let's go back up to the house. We can get you cleaned up and you can see her. I bet you've not had a decent meal in ages," she said, taking him by the hand.

She was so glad to see him again, though horrified by his story. The thought of Jenny's *daed* attacking Adam was too awful to contemplate, though it proved precisely why Elizabeth was far better off in Faith's Creek than in Philadelphia, and the thought strengthened her resolve to keep the *boppli* safe.

Gently, she led Adam up the path through the trees and through the garden gate, and up the path onto the porch. The smell of cooking wafted from the house, and she helped Adam take off his boots and step through the door into the kitchen where her *mamm* looked up from the stove in surprise.

"Oh, my, Leah! What's all this?" she asked.

Leah smiled. "This is Adam, *Mamm*," she replied.

Adam gave a weak smile and took off his hat.

With a bottle of witch hazel and some warm water, Leah and her *mamm* soon had Adam cleaned up. His injuries were superficial, though he would have some fine bruising on his cheeks, and dressed in some of Matthew's clothes he sat at the kitchen table playing with Elizabeth. The *boppli* who, though unable to express it in words, seemed delighted at having her *daed* back with her.

"You're very kind, and thank you for everything you've done for Elizabeth," Adam said, as Leah's mamm placed a dish of buttered noodles in front of him.

"We wouldn't have it any other way. She's family to us," she said, just as the porch door banged and Matthew entered the kitchen.

He too looked surprised to see Adam sitting at the table, and once again, the explanation was given as to Adam's presence. When Leah had finished, her *daed* looked at her with a grim expression, shaking his head, before sitting down heavily in a chair by the stove.

"I'm not happy about this, Leah. There's a lot of dangerous things going on. This man's brought that danger into my house, and he's brought it on all of us, too," he said, turning to Adam.

Color flushed up Adam's cheeks and he couldn't hold Matthew's gaze. "I'm sorry, I didn't mean to. This has all gotten out of hand," he began.

Leah's daed raised his hand to stop him. "You're right, son, it has, and you've led my daughter into it. We were happy to take care of Elizabeth. She's the innocent party in all of this. But what do you expect of us now?" he asked.

"I... I don't expect anything, I promise you. I just want what's best for Elizabeth. I wanted to see her, that's all," he said.

"A web of lies, that's what you've created, and I don't know what your intentions toward my daughter are, but I don't care for them," Matthew replied.

Leah looked imploringly at her *mamm*, hoping a word from her might calm the situation.

"Matthew, we need to help this young man, he's..." she began, but just then, Elizabeth opened her arms and gazed up at Adam with an adoring look.

"Daeda, Daeda," she murmured.

Leah gave an exclamation of surprise. "You said your first word," she cried, and Elizabeth laughed.

"Grossdaeda," she said, pointing at Leah's daed, whose hard countenance seemed to melt, his face breaking into a smile.

"Oh, would you hear that?" he said, a look of wonder on his face.

Leah smiled. "She's so happy here, *Daed*, and now that Adam's come, she'll be happier still. Can't he stay for a bit? He's been through so much, and all he wants is to make a home for Elizabeth. Isn't that what we've tried to do, too?" she said.

Matthew sighed. "All right, he can stay, but only until things settle down, and if any trouble comes this way, he's out. Do you hear me?" he said.

Leah nodded. "I hear you, *Daed*," she replied, glancing at Adam, who smiled.

"Thank you," he whispered, gazing lovingly down at Elizabeth, who repeated her earlier words proudly.

"Now, I think we could all do with a slice of Shoofly pie," Rebecca said, and it seemed that for now the matter of Adam and Elizabeth was settled.

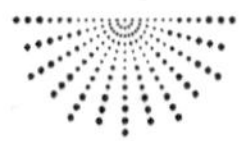

CHAPTER TWELVE

A week went by, and Adam's bruises soon healed. He was something like his old self again, and he delighted in spending time with Elizabeth, who in turned doted on her "daeda."

Leah, too, was happy, pleased to have Adam at her side, and feeling as though she had gained the family she had so long desired.

Word had soon spread around Faith's Creek of Adam's arrival, and Matthew was swift to point out that the young man from Philadelphia was sleeping in the attic room and that no impropriety was forthcoming.

"I don't want rumors spreading, Leah," he had told her.

Leah had assured him she and Adam would behave with the utmost integrity.

In fact, Leah was unsure where she stood with Adam. He doted on Elizabeth, and though he spoke of the importance of family and of raising Elizabeth the right way, he was yet to tell Leah how he felt about her. It created a strange situation, one which led Leah to question what it was that was between them – were they merely friends, was there something more, and what would the future hold?

"Your *daed* still seems distant with me," Adam said as he was picking up the language and customs. Even reading the Ordnung at times. "I offered to help him with the woodpile this morning and he plain refused. I don't know what I can do," Adam said.

They were sitting together on the porch drinking lemonade. Leah was holding Elizabeth in her arms, rocking her back and forth to coax her to sleep.

"He's a stubborn man, there's not a lot you can do to change him. It'll take time. The longer you stay, the easier it'll become," she replied.

Adam laughed. "I'll need to stay ten years for that," he said, and she smiled.

"I wouldn't mind that," she said, and he looked up at her and shook his head.

"I don't know, I don't know what I'll do next, where we'll go," he said.

The word "we," caused a lump to form in Leah's throat. The thought of him taking Elizabeth away with him was awful, and she shook her head, clinging tightly to the *boppli*, as though their departure was imminent.

"I prayed for you to come back," she said, reaching out her hand across the table and slipping it into his.

"I think your prayers worked," he replied.

"You're glad you found me, too – as well as Elizabeth?" she asked.

They had shared so much in the past, so much water under the bridge, and though her rumspringa seemed a distant memory, her feelings for Adam were as fresh as they had ever been. She loved him, and she had not stopped loving him in the months following her return to Faith's Creek. Their chance encounter in the park in Philadelphia was *Gott's* will, and it had seemed as though fate had decreed they should be together now.

"I am, of course, I am, I didn't stop thinking about you, either," he replied.

Relief washed over her and it felt like the first sun after the winter. Renewing, refreshing, and a hope for the future. "And what about now? Could you leave that old life behind and start again? You seem happy here, but it's not Philadelphia. What are you going to do?" she asked.

He sighed. "I don't know – what do you want me to do? I'm not sure what you want. This was only meant to be a temporary thing, at least until things settled down. I didn't expect you to be Elizabeth's *mamm*. Not really," he said.

She smiled. "But I want to be, and if you'll stay, I'd like that, too. I don't want to lose her, I don't want to lose you, either," she said.

He rose from his place and came to kneel down in front of her, gazing at Elizabeth cradled in her arms, then looking up into Leah's eyes and smiling.

"Can you forgive me for being a jerk?" he said.

She laughed. "You weren't. You just did what you thought was right – you were trying to help Jenny, I know that now," she said.

Leah had not held their first parting against him. She knew from bitter experience with Alma how feelings could change, and now she shook her head and leaned forward to kiss him on the forehead.

"But I didn't need to be so cold toward you, that's all. I treated you so badly, Leah. It was wrong of me," he said.

She shook her head. "Leave it in the past. It's the present that matters. And right now, we've got a *boppli* to take care of," she said, as Elizabeth began to squirm in her arms.

"We have if you're willing," he said, and Leah smiled.

"Together?" she said, and he nodded.

"Together, that's all I want, and if it's what you want, too, then I'm more than willing to share it," he said, leaning up to embrace her, as Leah felt a rush of happiness flood through her, and a sense that everything would now be all right.

*L*eah had her answer. She knew Adam loved her, that he had always loved her, and that only his doubts as to her feelings had held him back. They were each as bad as the other, believing that a parting of ways had meant a parting of feelings when in truth it had only led to those feelings strengthening. Leah could not have been happier, and she decided to confide in her *mamm*, though for now, she would have her promise not to reveal her and Adam's intentions to her *daed*.

"And you think you can trust him?" Rebecca asked as she stood with her hands deep in dough at the kitchen table later that day.

Adam had gone for a walk with Elizabeth, and Leah had taken the opportunity to explain to her *mamm* what had passed between them on the porch that morning.

"I think so, yes. He's a good man, and I love him," she replied.

Rebecca smiled. "Sometimes these out of towners, these blown ins... well, they're not used to our ways. They come to a place like Faith's Creek and yearn for more," she said.

"But don't some come and find just what they're looking for. Think of Sawyer. He left the community he lived in for his rumspringa and vowed never to come back, but now he's as Amish as... well as... you and Daed. Surely, it's about finding the right fit," she said.

Rebecca's eyebrows rose but then she smiled. "There's that, too, I admit," she replied.

"But why doesn't *Daed* like Adam? He's always so cold with him, and Adam tries his best. He offers to help. He makes himself useful without being asked. He's doing everything he can to fit in. But *Daed*... I don't know, it's as though he's already decided against Adam, and that's wrong. Judge not..." she said.

Her *mamm* sighed.

It seemed that whatever Adam did, he was in the wrong. Leah had tried her best to make him feel welcome, and so had her *mamm* – even going so far as to learn the recipe for Hoagie's, so that Adam might enjoy a taste of Philadelphia in Faith's Creek. But unless her *daed* could be persuaded as to Adam's good intentions – and his merits – there could be no hope of anything further between them. Leah knew her *daed* had to approve, and that without his approval, their prospects of a happy life were far diminished.

"Let me talk to him, we'll find a way. We just want you to be happy, Leah," she said.

Leah nodded.

She had heard those words before. Alma had said them, too, and while the sentiment was meant kindly, Leah wished others would allow her to decide what made her happy and accept it. She was happy as Elizabeth's *mamm*, and happier still, with Adam at her side. It may not have been the most conventional of courtships, but it certainly felt right, and Leah believed with all her heart that it was *Gott's* will that had brought her and Adam back together.

"I want to marry him, *Mamm,*" she said, as the clattering of footsteps on the porch suggested the return of Adam with Elizabeth.

"Then may *Gott* bless that hope, Leah," Rebecca replied, smiling, as she returned to her baking.

* * *

"DID YOU ENJOY YOUR WALK?" Leah asked as she cradled Elizabeth in her arms.

"We walked right up onto the heights. We could see the whole of Faith's Creek from there, couldn't we, Elizabeth?" Adam replied.

Elizabeth beamed at him waving her tiny fists. "Daeda," she whispered, and he smiled at her.

"There's my good girl, but I'm sure you're tired now," he said, as Leah laid her into the crib, which stood by the window in her bedroom.

Elizabeth slept with her at night, but sometimes, if she woke up early, Adam would take her down to the parlor and allow Leah a few more hours of sleep. It was tiring taking care of a *boppli* who had no idea of night and day and woke up as soon as she felt hungry. Leah yawned, smiling at Elizabeth, who gazed up at her and gurgled.

"That's right, you go to sleep now," she said, straightening up and turning to Adam, who was watching her with a smile on his face.

"You're such a good *mamm* to her, Leah, you really are. She loves you so much," he said, and he put his arms around her and kissed her on the forehead.

"And I love being her *mamm*, and I know you love being her *daed*. I just don't understand how anyone wouldn't want to take care of a precious little child like her. I feel so sorry for Jenny," she said.

Adam sighed. "She's got a lot of troubles. It's sad, but it's true. She couldn't take care of her, and the *daed* wanted nothing to do with her. It was all so tragic. I'm just glad she had the sense to realize her limitations. She asked me to help her. She didn't want her parents snatching Elizabeth away from her. She'd endured enough at their hands, and she wasn't about to let them take Elizabeth away, not for anything. I admired her for that. She wanted what was best for her daughter, even if it meant enduring the sorrow of separation," he replied.

"That's why I feel a double duty toward her. I feel like we've been trusted with a precious treasure, Adam, by Jenny, by *Gott*, by one another," she said, resting her head on his chest.

She could hear the gentle tapping of his heart, and in his arms, she felt at peace, protected from the outside world, their little family safe together. She needed nothing more than this, for, at last, she had what she had always longed for.

"And it's together we'll take care of her, I promise. We've been given an awesome responsibility, Leah, doubly, as you say. We owe it to Jenny, and to Elizabeth, to do our best by them," he said.

"We'll be all right, we've got each other," she replied, just as Elizabeth let out a gurgle, smiling up at the two of them from her crib, the parents who loved her, and who would do anything to protect her.

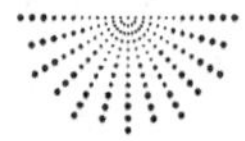

CHAPTER FOURTEEN

Miriam was holding Samuel in her arms. He was asleep, his perfect little features curled up, his thumb in his mouth, and she leaned forward and kissed him gently on the forehead.

"He's just perfect, Alma," she said, as Alma entered the parlor with a tray of coffee and cake.

"When he's asleep, he is," she replied, smiling, and shaking her head.

She poured out a cup of coffee for Miriam, before settling herself in a chair opposite and sighing. Alma's house was still somewhat chaotic. She and Sawyer had moved in a few weeks after the wedding after Bishop Beiler had pulled some strings with one of the farmers. It was a pretty little place, surrounded by a small garden which Sawyer had dug over for vegetables, and was perfect for two newlyweds.

"I think he is all the time," Miriam said, and Alma laughed.

"You try telling yourself that when he's crying at three o'clock in the morning," she said, offering Miriam a piece of seed cake.

"And now he's got a friend to play with. Isn't it adorable to see him and Elizabeth together? Two Philadelphia babies," Miriam said.

She had just come from visiting with Leah and Adam and had spent her time there, similarly in charge of a *boppli*.

"They play so nicely together. I know they're only small, but you can tell they're friends," she said.

"And they'll grow up together – now that Adam's staying in Faith's Creek. I'm so happy for Leah, she's finally found what she deserves," Miriam replied.

Leah had confided in Miriam and Alma as to what Adam had said, and how the two of them intended to settle down together in Faith's Creek. It had made them both happy to hear, knowing how much Leah had always desired a family of her own. It may not have come about in the usual manner, but Leah was happy and that was all that mattered.

"We've both had a strange way of going about marriage," Alma replied, shaking her head.

"When I find a man, I'm going to do things differently," Miriam said, and Alma raised her eyebrows and smiled.

"Is that so? Well, we don't always get to choose how life turns out, Miriam. I didn't exactly go to Philadelphia hoping to come back with a *boppli* belonging to someone else," she said, and Miriam blushed.

"I know, but..." she began, but Alma interrupted her.

"*Gott's* will, that's what matters. We have to follow where He leads us. Don't you think it was *Gott's* will that put me in Philadelphia at the right time and *Gott's* will that brought Leah and Adam together in the park? That's what having faith means, trusting in *Gott* to lead us along the right path – even if it's the unexpected one," she said, as Samuel started to cry.

Miriam rocked him in her arms, shushing him, and pondering Alma's words – did *Gott* really lead people in such a way, she wondered? She had grown up surrounded by people who trusted in just that way. It was a trust she wished she could grow into, too, one which seemed to give such hope and certainty to those around her – Alma and Leah included.

"Well... I still hope I find the man I'm looking for and I don't want to have to go to Philadelphia to find him, though I suppose if all our husbands came from there it would make a nice story," she said, handing Samuel back to Alma.

"Aren't you still desperate to go off on your rumspringa? When I went, you couldn't wait to follow. Have *bopplis* put you off Philadelphia forever?" Alma joked.

"No, I just want to do things my way. I still want to go on my rumspringa, though I suppose I might meet a husband here in Faith's Creek," she said.

Alma gave her a knowing smile. "You mean Jonathan Kemp?" she asked.

Miriam blushed.

In the weeks since Alma's wedding, Miriam and Jonathan had grown closer. In fact, they were due to go for a walk together that very day. Miriam glanced at the clock and gave an exclamation.

"Oh, I need to be going, I'm meeting him for a walk by the creek this afternoon. I lost track of the time," she said, rising hurriedly to her feet.

"He's a nice boy, you could do worse," Alma said.

"You mean to run off to Philadelphia and bring back a *boppli*?" Miriam replied with a chuckle.

Alma rolled her eyes. "You're on thin ice Miriam Graber," she said, smiling at her.

Miriam bid goodbye to Samuel, promising to return to see him very soon, and Alma followed her out onto the porch to wave her off.

"Do you think Leah's all right now?" she asked.

Alma nodded. "I think she's found her happiness. Adam's a good man, at least I think he is – he's come back, hasn't he, and Sawyer says..." she replied, her words trailing off.

"Sawyer?" Miriam asked.

"Oh, yes, they met in Philadelphia, quite by chance, you understand. He thinks Adam's all right. Anyway, you'd best hurry. We don't want you being late for Jonathan now, do we?" she replied.

Miriam made her way down the porch steps and across the garden, pausing at the gate to wave.

"I'll call by tomorrow or the day after. I've been making a blanket for Samuel, it's like Joseph's coat of many colors," she said, and Alma smiled and waved back.

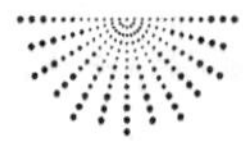

Jonathan was waiting for Miriam by the path which led to the creek. He smiled when he saw her coming and held out a small bag for her as she came to greet him.

"I got you something," he said, smiling at her.

"What's this?" she exclaimed, peering inside the bag, her face breaking into a smile.

"I know you like chocolate," he said, as she pulled out a large bar of Hershey's.

"I *love* chocolate," she said, thinking back to Philadelphia and the sight of the stores piled high with all manner of sweet delights.

"Shall we walk by the creek? I wouldn't mind a piece of that myself," he said, as Miriam pulled off the wrapping and broke off two squares.

He offered her his arm and the two of them made their way down the path which led through the woods and to the water's edge. Miriam had been unsure about Jonathan at first. He had seemed so overly keen, so intense in his attentions, but she had come to appreciate his kindness. His thoughtful gifts always made her smile, such as the bar of her favorite chocolate, and the normalness he represented, in contrast to the chaotic nature of Alma and Leah's search for love. Miriam knew her parents approved of Jonathan – they thought him a respectable young man from a good family, and she could picture herself growing old with him, happy in a marriage as conventional as that of her *mamm* and *daed*.

"I went to see the *bopplis*, today," she said, as they paused by the water's edge, and she broke off another two squares of chocolate for them.

"How were they? Growing up fast, I bet," he replied.

She nodded. "Samuel, especially. He's so big now, and he looks just like Sawyer," she said, smiling at the thought of Samuel gurgling and laughing in her arms earlier that afternoon.

"I suppose you want one now," he said.

Miriam blushed. "Perhaps... but I don't want one like that," she replied.

Miriam loved the thought of being a *mamm*. She wanted nothing else but that, though if she was going to have a *boppli*, she wanted it to be her own.

She knew that Alma and Leah doted on their children, but they were still not entirely theirs. Samuel was the child of a woman who had died, and Elizabeth the daughter of a woman who might return at any time – not to mention the grandparents seeking custody.

Adam was not even the true father of the child, and Miriam was sure there were legal ramifications to that. Her two friends had chosen such complicated means of achieving the families they desired, and though Miriam knew that neither of them had sought it, it seemed that *Gott* had led them both down a complicated path.

"You mean from Philadelphia?" he asked.

"Exactly, I don't want to bring someone else's boppli back to Faith's Creek from Philadelphia," she replied, smiling at him, and shaking her head.

They sat down on a tree stump next to the water's edge, and Jonathan picked up a stone and skimmed it over the water, where it bounced half a dozen times before falling with a splash into the deep.

"Are you worried about them? Your friends, I mean. Alma seems happy enough, she's married, and Leah's found Adam – he seems decent," Jonathan said.

Miriam sighed. "I just worry about the future. These *bopplis*, they're going to grow up asking questions. They're going to want to know where they came from, and what about when Leah and Alma have other children, too? Will they feel differently about them?" she asked.

Jonathan shrugged his shoulders and didn't seem to care. But Miriam was worried about both her friends, particularly Leah. There were still so many unanswered questions, and at any moment, Jenny's parents might find them, demanding custody of the grandchild that was rightfully theirs and their daughter's.

"I don't know. It's not exactly a conventional situation. I suppose only time will tell," he replied, glancing at the bar of chocolate that Miriam held in her hands.

She broke off another two pieces, and they sat munching for a moment in silence. Jonathan picked up another stone and skimmed it over the water, and Miriam watched as the ripples spread out across the pool. It was just the same for Leah and Adam – a splash with ripples going out, affecting everything with one single action.

"Anyway, I know one thing – I don't want a *boppli* from out of nowhere," she said, and he laughed.

"Well, I don't know, are you planning to find one in Philadelphia?" he asked, smiling at her.

"I don't know if I even want to go there, now. I was so set on my rumspringa, but now I've seen what's happened to Leah and Alma, what they've been through – is it worth it?" she asked.

"Isn't the point of a rumspringa to work out if this life is the right one for you? I enjoyed mine and love a little freedom sometimes, Still, I chose this life instead, and that's that," he replied.

"And you've far fewer troubles than Leah and Alma, that's for certain," she replied.

"I suppose so. My point is, you've got to follow your heart. If you want to go on a rumspringa then go, if not, stay," he said, slipping his hands into hers.

She rested her head on his shoulder, enjoying just being with him here in this moment. Life seemed simpler with Jonathan – far simpler than the lives which either Leah or Alma had built for themselves. Miriam had grown up believing she would meet a man like Jonathan, marry and settle down, have children and live a simple life. It was what so many others around her did, and though she had sometimes thought differently, she had come to see that such simplicity had its merits.

"What I want is not to be shocked by *bopplis* from out of nowhere, or men with more questions around them than answers. A man like you," she said, causing him to blush.

It was meant as a joke, though there was no denying the truth in it. The more time she spent with Jonathan, the more Miriam liked him – not because he was different, but because he was safe.

"I don't think I've got any hidden *bopplis*," he replied, and she laughed, gazing up into his eyes with a smile.

"Then that makes me happy," she replied, offering him another square of chocolate.

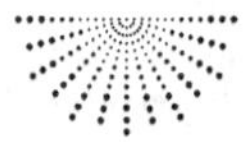

CHAPTER SIXTEEN

Elizabeth was crying. She had been grouchy all morning, and whether laid down or sitting up, Leah simply could not get her to settle. Finally, she had given up trying to get the *boppli* to sleep and instead had taken her down to the parlor to sit with her by the stove. Both her *mamm* and *daed* were out – her *mamm* at the market, and her *daed* having gone for a walk with Adam in an attempt to forge a bond between them.

Leah was pleased with the effort he was finally making, and though she could not get Elizabeth to settle, she was grateful that at last family life seemed to be settling down. She had just got Elizabeth quiet when a knock came at the door, and she looked up to find Sarah Beiler on the porch, smiling at her through the glass panel.

"Oh, I'm pleased to see you," she exclaimed, opening the door, and balancing Elizabeth in her other hand as she did so.

"I thought I'd come and pay you a visit, it's been a week or so since I last saw you. How's Elizabeth?" Sarah asked, stepping inside and putting her hand gently on Elizabeth's head.

"She's growing bigger by the moment, but I can't settle her this morning. She's grouchy about something or other," Leah replied, inviting Sarah to sit down.

"They have days like that. She'll be all right," Sarah replied.

"My parents are out – my *daed's* gone for a walk with Adam. I'm so pleased they're starting to get along now," Leah said.

Sarah smiled. "It takes Matthew time to trust, especially where his precious daughter is concerned, but you've made the right decision. Adam's fitting in so well in Faith's Creek, no one says a bad word about him. For a newcomer, an *Englischer*, he's doing well," she said.

It was true, Adam had fitted in well to the community, and Leah had been surprised by how easily he had come to settle down after the hustle and bustle of life in Philadelphia. Faith's Creek was quite a contrast, but Adam was making every effort to be helpful, and even her *daed* had admitted to warming to him.

"My *mamm* thinks he's wonderful, and I hope my *daed* comes to see that, too – he loves Elizabeth so much," Leah replied.

"And he loves you, too. The three of you make the perfect family, and after all, you've been through, you deserve a little happiness together. I'm sure your *daed* can see that Adam's serious about this and wants to make a go of things. Faith's Creek is all the better for having you all here. Sometimes we need reminding there's a world beyond this one, and a man like Adam does just that. Do you pray with him?" she asked.

Leah thought for a moment. She and Adam had not much discussed matters of faith, though she knew he believed. They had not prayed together, and she wondered why – there was no reason why they should not have done. The blush that came over her face answered the question.

"I don't know why we haven't – we should have done," she said.

Sarah smiled. "You'd be surprised how many couples don't, but if you're going to marry, then it's an important way to prepare. The family that prays together, stays together, that's what I always say," she said.

Leah nodded. "I just hope my *daed* and Adam can put their differences behind them," she replied, as the sound of footsteps on the porch announced the return of her family.

A moment later, Adam and Matthew entered the house, followed by her *mamm* who had returned from the market at the same moment as her *daed* and Adam got home.

"Oh, how nice to see you, Sarah," Rebecca said, setting down her basket, "will you stay for something to eat?"

Leah eyed her *daed* somewhat nervously. He was a hard character to read, and she wondered what had transpired between him and Adam on their walk. Elizabeth was asleep now, and Leah rose to peer inside the crib, smiling at the sight of the sleeping infant, so peaceful with her well-chewed teddy bear in her arms.

"She went straight off as soon as we started talking," Leah said, smiling at Sarah as if her presence was magical.

"Let's try and keep her asleep a while longer, at least until we've eaten," Adam said.

Soon, the table was laid, and the pies which Rebecca had brought from the market were in the oven, a pleasing smell wafted through the house. Leah and Sarah helped peel the potatoes, and Adam was set to work peeling carrots and turnips to boil and mash.

"I think things will be ok with your *daed*," Adam whispered, as he and Leah stood next to each other at the stove watching the pots. At the table, Sarah and Rebecca shared news from the market.

"It wasn't awkward or anything, was it?" she replied, and he shook his head.

"He just wanted to know more about me. We hadn't had a chance to talk before – not alone. I think we'll be all right. He's been to Philadelphia," Adam said.

Leah looked at him in amazement. "Philadelphia? My *daed*?" she asked, just as her *mamm* called them to the table.

"All right, I think it's all ready now, come sit down," she said before Adam had a chance to explain further.

Leah thought back to the previous week. There had been one day when her *daed* had absented himself, but he had told her he was going to Bird-in-Hand to see about some livestock. He must have gone to Philadelphia then, but why?

She took her place at the table opposite Adam, glancing at her *daed*, who now bowed his head in prayer.

"A short moment of silence to give thanks for *Gott's* bounty," he said, and all of them bowed their heads to pray.

"Denke," Sarah said, a few moments later, "you're very nice to invite me to stay."

"It's the least we could do. You've been so kind to Leah, and it was you who reminded us of our Christian duty toward Elizabeth," Rebecca said, as she began to serve out the pies and potatoes.

"We're grateful to you, Sarah, we really are," Matthew said.

Leah watched him keenly, desperate to ask him what had happened in Philadelphia, and what had prompted his apparent change of mind toward Adam.

"This is delicious," Adam said, thanking Rebecca, who had given him an extra-large portion of the pie.

"Well, I know you've got a good appetite, you're just like Matthew used to be. A man should have a good appetite, I always say," she said, smiling at Adam who thanked her again.

"We walked right up onto the heights this afternoon. I never tire of seeing that view across the state, it's just beautiful, isn't it?" Matthew said, helping himself from the dish of mashed carrots and turnip.

"We should take the buggy up there one time and have a picnic. Elizabeth would love that, I'm sure," Leah said, and her *daed* nodded.

"The three of you could go together, you, Adam, and Elizabeth," he said, smiling at Leah.

"I'd like that – would you mind us going alone?" she asked, and Matthew shook his head.

"I suppose I'd better tell you – and I'm pleased you're here, too Sarah – that Adam and I have had a little talk," he said, glancing at Adam, who nodded.

"We've cleared the air," Adam said, and he slipped his hand into Leah's and smiled.

"I wasn't at the livestock auction in Bird-in-Hand last week. I went to Philadelphia, instead. I wanted to find a few things out for myself. I had a lot of questions," Matthew said.

Leah's heart skipped a beat, and she glanced at Adam, who smiled.

"It's all right, your *daed's* right – I came with a lot of unanswered questions attached," he said.

Matthew chuckled at the understatement. "Well, that's right. I wanted to know the truth. I was worried about you, Leah, and I had to know we weren't all of us heading for disaster. So I went to Philadelphia, and I saw Elizabeth's family for myself – don't worry, I didn't speak to them, they don't know me, but I did speak to a neighbor of theirs, and he told me some pretty terrible things. Like how Jenny's *daed* was arrested for assault only last month, and how the neighborhood's gone downhill since they moved in. They said it was one disaster after another, and I vowed there and then that my grand... yes, my grand-daughter, well, she's not going to grow up there. She's staying right here with the people who love her, and that includes Adam. It's no wonder he wanted to keep Elizabeth safe, and I understand everything he did now," he said, turning to Adam, and holding out his hand.

Leah watched as Adam and her *daed* shook hands, and a tear rolled down her cheek at the sight which she knew meant a new chapter was beginning for them all.

"So, he can stay?" she asked.

Matthew nodded. "He certainly can, and what's more, a blessing on the three of you," he replied, as Leah squeezed Adam's hand, and right on cue Elizabeth woke up!

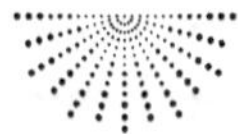

*L*ater that day, when Sarah Beiler had left, and Rebecca was seeing to Elizabeth, Leah and Adam stepped out onto the porch and took a walk together in the garden.

Gone was the tension of the previous weeks, replaced with a sense that the future would be one of harmony and grace for them all. Leah had not felt so happy in a long time, and the thought of them all being together as a family was a delight.

"It's all worked out all right, hasn't it?" she said, slipping her arm into Adam's and resting her head on his shoulder.

"There'll be some difficulties ahead – there's still the question of custody – but we'll face it together, and there's no doubt Elizabeth is in the right place. We've done what's best for her, and we've found each other again in the process," Adam replied.

"As a family," she said, and he nodded.

"I feel safe here, too. I wish I'd come sooner. I don't know what held me back," he said, but she smiled up at him and shook her head.

"Things happen for a reason, *Gott's* purposes can be hard to see sometimes. All of this happened for a reason: to bring Elizabeth safely to where she belongs. If you'd come sooner, she might have been taken away from us. But now, she's safe, and that's all that matters, and we're together, too," she replied.

"I will have to be accepted into the church. I know there is a lot of work for me to do to get there," he said.

"I will help you and I'm sure Sarah and Amos Beiler will champion your cause. With the bishop on your side, you have every reason to be accepted."

"I hope so," he said.

"Have faith," she replied.

"You're right, I do, but there's still something I need to ask you," he said, and her heart skipped a beat.

She had hoped the question was coming – it was asked in action, if not in word – but to hear him say it – that was a very different thing, indeed. They were beneath the laurel trees at the far end of the garden, the sweet scent of eucalyptus and roses on the breeze, and he turned to her, taking her by the hand and gazing down at her with a loving look in his eyes.

"If it's truly what you want," she whispered, and he nodded.

"And if it's what you want, too, Leah, then that's all that matters. I should have asked you this a long time ago, but... will you marry me?" he asked.

Leah had known the question was coming, but the delight in hearing it was not lessened by the anticipation. There was only one answer she could give, and she threw arms around him and kissed him.

"I will," she whispered, as tears rolled down her cheeks. "I just have one question. Will you pray with me sometime?"

A big smile crossed his face. "I have been wanting to ask you the same thing but was embarrassed to do so. I was afraid you would think my prayers were unworthy."

Leah swatted his arm. "Silly, talking to Gott is never silly, how you do it may be different but we are all different and that is Gott's glorious will. I can't wait."

Adam pulled her close and kissed her very gently.

Just then, Elizabeth's cries came from the house, and footsteps on the porch caused them to turn.

"Leah, Adam, come quickly – she just said another word. Oh, it's just adorable," Rebecca called out.

"What did she say?" Leah asked, and Rebecca smiled.

"She's asking for her *mamma* and *daeda*, I think she means the two of you..." she said, and with a smile on their faces, Leah and Adam walked hand in hand back to the house, each knowing the joy of love and family together.

* * *

IF YOU MISSED Love and Faith grab it here

Love and
FAITH

Anna Sutter had a good life, all things considered. *Gott* had graced her with a loving *mamm* and *daed,* and a younger *schweschder* who seemed to shine as brightly as the sun.

When there were so many people in the world who had not even one person to care for them, she knew that she was blessed beyond measure. That was what made her pervasive sadness all the more difficult to bear.

She lived in an Amish community called Faith's Creek, along with the rest of her *familye.* It was the place she had been born, as had her parents before her. She had *nee* doubt at all that it would be where she lived still when it was finally time for her to go to be with *Gott.*

She thought it was probably one of the loveliest places in all of the world, although she had nothing to compare it to, and she was happy enough to stay there for the whole of her life. It wasn't where she was that made her unhappy, it was who she was inside, and she thought that must be a good deal worse.

She was a slight young woman, slender trending on the side of frail. Her deep chestnut hair was always up under the covering of her *kapp*. She was careful never to let a single strand stray out of place if she could help it. She did not like the idea of giving people a reason for her to be seen.

Her eyes were wide and almost as dark as her hair, and her skin was as pale as a fresh container of cream. Against the dark hues of the blue dresses that were her daily uniform, she worried that the extremity of her fairness made her stand out like a white sheet fluttering across a night-darkened sky. The thought alone made her tremble with dread, and it made her more than a little weary to venture outdoors more than was strictly necessary.

Perhaps worst of the long list of things she believed weren't quite right about her, was the fact that at twenty-years-old, she remained unwed. Not only was she still unmarried, when many of her peers had already begun their own happy *familye's,* but she also had nary a prospect or hope of being courted anytime soon. It seemed to her that, aside from her always loving parents and *schweschder,* nobody in Faith's Creek wanted her or would really care if she were suddenly gone.

"Such a foolish way to think," she chastised herself as she tugged mercilessly at her needle and thread. "Such a waste of energy. What does it matter if you're wanted by others at all? You contribute. You work as hard as you can to help make this *haus* a home."

She nodded to herself, glancing down at the ever-growing pile of completed mending beside her for reassuring proof. It was true that she was a hard worker, and one who never complained, and she knew her parents appreciated that about her.

Unfortunately, it was also true that if she were never able to find a man who wanted to take her for his *fraa,* she would undoubtedly prove to be a burden as her parents moved into their golden years of age. They would have to continue to care for her long past the point when parents were meant to be relieved of that task. The mere thought of it was enough to make her shudder, and her eyes well up with tears.

"*Ach*, here you are!" Anna's *schweschder*, Ruth, exclaimed from the open screen door of the back porch. "I've been looking for you all over. I thought you had gone and disappeared."

"*Nee*, I've been right here the whole time," Anna protested, her heart hammering in her chest as she tried in vain to recover from her start. "And you frightened me half to death. You shouldn't sneak up on people like that, Ruth. You really shouldn't."

"I know," Ruth said with a dramatic sigh that wasn't quite able to make up for the glint of mischief shining in her cornflower eyes. "But sometimes, I just can't seem to help myself. And, anyway, I really was looking for you, and for what felt like the longest time. Have you been out here all day?"

"Why, I don't know," Anna answered with a small frown of confusion.

She looked out from beneath the porch's comfortably weathered ceiling and gazed up at the sky, trying to determine what time it was. Truth be told, she didn't have the first clue how long she had been out there on her own. That was one of the hazards of being a person who spent most of her waking hours on her own. Time had a way of losing itself, and sometimes, of disappearing altogether.

"Well, I think you have been," Ruth said decisively, her hands on her hips as she surveyed Anna's day's work with a scrutinizing eye. "And I think it's enough for today. It's time to put your work away, too."

"*Ach,* really?" Anna asked, laughing despite herself. "And what brought you to that conclusion?"

"My keen powers of observation," Ruth said, her expression kept serious for only a moment before she collapsed into a fit of giggles that Anna couldn't help but join in.

And that was the thing about Ruth, the thing that everybody who met her couldn't help but notice. Ruth was the sort of girl that people just wanted to be around, even if they couldn't quite put their finger on why. She was funny and kind, silly, and a little bit wild, and all of those things were absolutely contagious.

In short, Anna believed that her sweet, sixteen-year-old *schweschder* was all of the things that she herself was not. Whereas Anna was likely to blend seamlessly into the background of any gathering she was forced to attend, Ruth was always like a bright, shining star in a crowd.

Everyone wanted to be around her, and although she was still just a little bit too young to begin a courtship, it was already widely understood who she would eventually marry. It was understood with a confidence that Anna couldn't remember ever having about anything in her life.

Ruth and a boy named Jonathan Knepp had been thick as thieves for as long as anyone could remember, and their friendship seemed to be naturally evolving into something far deeper. While Jonathan was about to leave for his *Rumspringa,* people expected that when he returned to Faith's Creek, he and Ruth would begin courting. They would be wed, and Anna would officially be surpassed by her lovely younger *schweschder.*

"I'm serious, Anna," she whined now, reaching for Anna's hand and trying to tug her onto her feet. "It's time to put this away. Don't you want to have a little bit of adventure in your life?"

"What?" Anna asked with surprise and not a little bit of dread. "*Nee,* of course not. What are you going on about, anyhow?"

"Nothing," Ruth answered, a pretty pout on her pert, sixteen-year-old lips. "I'm just saying that it might not be such a bad thing for you to do something other than work and shut yourself away in the *haus*."

"It's a *wunderbaar haus*," Anna snapped back, her tone more severe than she intended, although she didn't seem to make it otherwise. "And I don't mind the work. I'm happy to do it. I'm happy to be useful to our parents. I think they need me to do what I do, anyhow. What would they think if I just ran off?"

"They would be pleased for you to have a little time to yourself," Ruth answered immediately, and with a confidence that Anna didn't think she had ever felt before in her life. "I was talking to *Mamm*..."

"About me?" Anna interrupted, finally getting to her feet as Ruth had wanted her to all along. "The two of you were talking about me without me being there?"

"*Jah*, but not anything bad," Ruth insisted, finally showing the faintest hint of uncertainty. "I was telling her that I wished the two of us spent more time together. Time outside of the *haus*, and she said she thought that was a lovely idea. She is the one who bade me come and find you. She told me you should come with me to game night."

That stopped Anna cold. The idea that two of the people she loved most in the world had come together to speak about the extent to which she was isolating herself made her feel exposed and ashamed. It was the very feeling she feared most, and so she kept herself apart as if it might keep her safe.

And yet, at the same time, there was a part of her that saw what Ruth was saying now as an opportunity. She saw it as a chance being offered to her, one that she was sorely tempted to take. Perhaps she wasn't destined to live out her days alone, after all, as unlikely as the possibility seemed. Maybe forcing herself to come out of her shell a little would offer her one of *Gott's* many blessings and rewards.

"*Jah,*" she said softly before she had time to convince herself not to speak at all.

"What?" Ruth asked, her eyes growing wide with disbelief. "What did you say?"

"I said *Jah,*" Anna repeated, smiling at her *schweschder's* obvious delight despite the butterflies fluttering wildly in her stomach. "All right. I'll accompany you into town tonight, just so long as you promise not to try and turn it into a habit."

Instead of answering, Ruth threw her arms around Anna's neck. Anna understood that Ruth's failure to agree to her terms meant that there would likely be similar requests in the future. At the moment, however, she found that she didn't really care. She was going to allow herself an adventure, and despite it being a small one, she was excited for what may come to pass.

Grab Amish Love in Faith's Creek a super value 15 Book Box Set now for FREE with Kindle Unlimited.

Find all Sarah's books on Amazon and click the yellow follow button

This book is dedicated to the wonderful Amish people and the faithful life that they live.

Go in peace my friends.

As an independent author, Sarah relies on your support. If you enjoyed this book, please leave a review on Amazon or Goodreads.

ABOUT THE AUTHOR

Sarah Miller was born in Pennsylvania and spent her childhood close to the Amish people. Weekends were spent doing chores; quilting or eventually babysitting in the community. She grew up to love their culture and the simple lifestyle and had many Amish friends. The one thing that you can guarantee when you are near the Amish, Sarah believes is that you will feel close to God.

Many years later she married Martin who is the love of her life and moved to England. There she started to write stories about the Amish. Recently after a lot of persuasion from her best friend she has decided to publish her stories. They draw on inspiration from her relationship with the Amish and with God and she hopes you enjoy reading them as much as she did writing them. Many of the stories are based on true events but names have been changed and even though they are authentic at times artistic license has been used.

Sarah likes her stories simple and to hold a message and they help bring her closer to her faith. She currently lives in Yorkshire, England with her husband Martin and seven very spoiled chickens.

She would love to meet you on Facebook at https://www.facebook.com/SarahMillerBooks

Sarah hopes her stories will both entertain and inspire and she wishes that you go with God.

www.ingramcontent.com/pod-product-compliance
Lightning Source LLC
Chambersburg PA
CBHW071519150726
48000CB00002B/613